DEACON

TED WOODS

Beaten Track
www.beatentrackpublishing.com

Deacon

First published 2024 by Beaten Track Publishing

Paperback ISBN: 978 1 78645 646 5
eBook ISBN: 978 1 78645 647 2

Cover Photography by Anne Taylor and David Holroyd

Beaten Track Publishing,
Burscough, Lancashire.
www.beatentrackpublishing.com

Dedicated with love and thanks to my wife Anne,
who will mark the 30th anniversary of being made a deacon
on 19th June 2024.

Thanks also to Debbie McGowan of Beaten Track Publishing
for her advice and support.

The characters in this novel are fictitious and are not intended to bear resemblance to anyone living or dead.
The church structures are those of the Church of Ireland, but these are just context and are not intended to reflect on any office holders or parishes.

Chapter 1

IT WAS THE last evensong of the Michaelmas term in the Church of Ireland Theological Institute. The service would be followed by Christmas Dinner in the dining room, and then, when the dining room had been cleared, the annual staff and students' Christmas party was to be held.

The students' social committee had decided that this year's party would consist of a 'Vicars and Tarts' night. A selection of drinks had been bought and a band booked. Costumes were laid out in the students' room ready for wearing after dinner.

There was a frivolous atmosphere at evensong, which wasn't helped by the students leading the service. With the forthcoming party in mind, instead of two solemn Advent hymns, they chose 'Yield Not to Temptation' and 'Do No Sinful Action'.

There were titters all round as the hymns were announced, and even the director, sitting in the back pew of the college chapel, couldn't help smiling.

But not everyone was amused. Jonathan Appleford, a third-year student and leader of the evangelical group, stormed into the vestry after the service to confront the two celebrants.

"You have made a mockery of tonight's service with your childish attempt at humour," he fumed. "It's nothing short of sacrilegious. I have a good mind to take this to the college council, but as it's the last service of the term and we're having a party tonight, I'll leave it for this time. But you have been warned."

"Oh, come on, Jonathan, it was only a bit of fun. Lighten up, for heaven's sake!"

"I don't regard divine service as the place for levity and fun. We're a church not a music hall," he said stiffly and left the room.

"Nor, it seems, is there any fun in being a fundamentalist," one of the students remarked to another.

Jonathan Appleford was in his final year at the Theological Institute training to be ordained. He was twenty-four years old, tall, slim, fresh-faced and good-looking but very serious. He seldom smiled, and when he did, it looked more like a condescending smirk. He never attended the weekly 'Vestry meetings' in the snug of the local pub where most of the students socialised on Wednesday evenings. He was more likely to be part of the college prayer group, beseeching God that those in the pub would see the error of their ways and amend their ungodly lives.

Brought up in a strict evangelical church-going Northern Ireland family, Jonathan had never kicked over the traces. A member of Scripture Union at school and the Christian Union at university, he was ever 'sober, steadfast and demure', ever-vigilant in renouncing the temptations of the world, the flesh and the devil.

He was born in 1998, the year The Good Friday Agreement had been signed. Its signing heralded the dawn of peace after thirty years of violence in Northern Ireland. As a city, Belfast was transformed. Night life thrived once again. Pubs and restaurants opened up in streets and alleys that were avoided even in daytime during the Troubles. The city always seemed to be constantly en fête, but Jonathan never sampled any of its delights.

He kept strictly within his own area in suburban Belfast and to the activities of his home church. Even when he was at Queen's

University, he was never part of the pub and restaurant culture of the nearby Lisburn Road.

After graduating from Queen's, he went to train for ministry in the Church of Ireland Theological Institute in Dublin. His only forays into the city centre were to attend lectures in Trinity College. Every weekend, he travelled home to be part of his local church. When it came to doing an internship in his final year, he chose a parish in his home diocese, which was noted for its conservatism. He was determined not to have anything to do with anyone or anywhere that could be described as Liberal Catholic or even 'liberal'!

Chapter 2

IT WAS A surprise to many, both in the institute and in his home diocese, that Jonathan did not take a curacy in his home diocese but rather accepted the offer of the Venerable Guy Morgan to become curate of St. Stephen's, Lislea, in the diocese of Daneford, not far from Dublin.

For a strict conservative curate like Jonathan, the archdeacon had all the right credentials. He had made a name for himself in Church Growth circles in England. Head-hunted by the previous bishop, he had lost little time in making sure that St. Stephen's had the name of being a lively, growing parish with an active youth ministry. Guy Morgan was not fussy about liturgical formalities. He had introduced a worship band and all the latest audiovisual technology. *And sure*, Jonathan thought to himself as he considered Guy's offer of a curacy in St. Stephen's, *don't the liberal, cultural Protestants of the Republic need converting anyway?*

The appointment had been made in March, six months before his priesting and the start of his curacy.

The director of the Theological Institute had her reservations about the appointment. She felt that Jonathan desperately needed to expand his understanding of the broad nature of Anglicanism and, accordingly, arranged a meeting with him in her office.

"I've been thinking about your parish experience and ministerial development," she said. "I know your home church is very like what you will meet when you start your curacy with Archdeacon Morgan in St. Stephen's. Also, your deacon's year placement has been in a similar church setting. Before going to your curacy, I think you'd benefit from something different in terms of churchmanship and theology, just to give you a more rounded view of Anglicanism.

"I have contacts in some of the English theological colleges, and I know they are interested in doing some student exchanges. Would you agree to go on such an exchange for the summer term? All your essays and projects have been completed, so an exchange would not interfere with your degree work. What do you think? It can be easily arranged."

"Well, yes, if you think it would be of benefit," replied Jonathan, a little flattered he'd been chosen.

"You will still get your student grant, and your stay, of course, will be free. The institute will pay all your travel expenses—I can tap a bursary for a top-up for living expenses. I'm sure it will be a most formative time, and it will always look good on your CV as you progress through your ministry."

A few weeks later, feeling like a young schoolboy about to start his first term in boarding school, Jonathan arrived with his cases at the front door of the theological college which was to be his home for the next ten weeks. It was an imposing red-brick building which fronted a busy street in the heart of Cambridge.

The college was expecting him, and he was shown to the rooms that had been allocated to him. There was a study/sitting room and a bedroom, both of which dated back to the college's foundation in the late-nineteenth century. The rooms felt cold and the furniture was antiquated. There were none of the modern facilities like an en-suite bathroom that he had had in the institute in Dublin. Toilet and washing facilities were shared in a large bathroom located on each floor.

But his room, on the third floor, had a stunning view of the college lawn, and Jonathan realised that behind the street façade, two wings extended at right angles to encompass the college garden, which was in full sunlight.

Not long after he'd finished unpacking, there was a knock on the door and the head student, Duncan Smith-Elliott, introduced himself and offered to take Jonathan on a tour of the college.

"Not all the lectures are held on site," he said as they started off. "We have to visit other colleges for some of them, so you'll need to familiarise yourself with where they are. A bicycle is the handiest form of travel. And, by the way, whereas we don't wear academic gowns to lectures here in the college, we are expected to wear them when visiting other colleges." The director of the institute had warned Jonathan of this, and he had packed his borrowed gown.

Duncan took Jonathan to the dining room, the lecture rooms and then to the common room, which, Jonathan was shocked to see, had a well-stocked bar along one wall.

"I suppose in Dublin, you had a daily routine to college life. Here, we start at seven-thirty a.m. with morning prayer, which is followed by Mass."

Mass! Jonathan felt his Ultra-Protestant hackles rise but decided at this stage not to protest.

"After Mass," Duncan continued, "we have breakfast, and then there are lectures here or at other colleges. You'll find the programme on the noticeboard in the main hall. I'm not sure which ones you will be attending. You'll need to discuss that with the principal. Lunch follows midday prayers, which, incidentally, are not compulsory. A bell rings seven times for services you are expected to attend and three times for optional services. There are more lectures and seminars in the afternoon. Evensong is at five-thirty p.m. and then dinner. Compline is at nine p.m."

Noticing that Jonathan was struggling to remember everything, Duncan smiled.

"You'll soon get used to the routine. Everyone finds it confusing to start with. But just to say that we begin each term with a one-day retreat. That will be tomorrow. It's being led by a retired bishop who lives in Cambridge. It's silence all day until after compline.

"Oh, just to warn you, there's no food in the college until tomorrow. A few of us are going to have a pint and something to eat in the pub tonight. You're very welcome to join us and meet some of the students."

Having avoided going to the 'vestry meetings' at the institute on principle, Jonathan had never been in a pub in his life.

"I think I'll give it a miss," he said, quickly adding, "but thank you for the offer. I'm pretty tired after the journey, so I'll have an early night."

"Fair enough," said Duncan. "There's a small kitchen at the end of the corridor if you want to make yourself something simple. Anyway, I'm afraid I have to go, so I'll say goodbye until tomorrow. Nice to have you with us. I hope you'll enjoy your stay."

After Duncan left, Jonathan set about retracing their tour of the college to familiarise himself with the layout. Other students were returning for the summer term, which Duncan had told him was the 'Easter term' in Cambridge. Laden with cases and rucksacks, they all seemed intent on getting to their rooms in preparation for the start of term and took no notice of him.

Coming back up the stairs to his room on the top floor, he found the kitchen and made himself a cup of coffee, which he took back with him.

Tired from travel and trying to come to terms with the very new experience of a term in one of Cambridge's theological colleges, he lay back on the bed and fell fast asleep, only to be wakened by the continuous ringing of a bell summoning him to worship the following morning.

Chapter 3

For Jonathan, the next few days felt like walking through a fog. Nothing was familiar and he wasn't sure what to expect next.

In the Irish system of training, students were ordained to the diaconate in their third and final year. When the principal of his adopted college heard that Jonathan was a deacon, he made sure that Jonathan would act as such for the first community eucharist of the term.

Thursday was designated a 'Community Night' in the college. Mass at five-thirty p.m. was followed by dinner, then drinks in the common room until compline at nine p.m., all of which filled Jonathan with fear and foreboding, feelings which were confirmed when, on the afternoon of being deacon at the Mass, he attended the chapel for a rehearsal.

As well as Jonathan, there was a sub-deacon, a censer, a crucifer and two acolytes. Jonathan hadn't a clue what he was supposed to do.

"Of course, you'll wear a dalmatic," said the sub-deacon, who was in charge of the rehearsal.

Jonathan had never even heard of such a vestment. He had only ever worn a cassock, surplice and scarf at every service. He and some of his fellow evangelicals didn't even approve of coloured stoles.

"Er, what's a dalmatic?" he asked, adding, to excuse his ignorance, "We aren't very high church in Dublin."

The sub-deacon raised his eyes to heaven. "It's the vestment that is worn by the deacon over the alb. It has wide sleeves and is made of brocade in the seasonal colour. It is a bit like a chasuble, which is worn by the celebrant. As sub-deacon, I will wear a tunicle, which is shorter."

"OK! Got you," said Jonathan, still mystified.

"Now can we get this rehearsal going?" the sub-deacon said impatiently. "Let's practise the procession. Line up. James, you are the crucifer, Mark and Rose, you are the acolytes. Will you please keep pace with one another? Mark and Rose, keep your candles level!

The sub-deacon looked at Jonathan sceptically. "I will look after the thurible this time. Jonathan, you will carry the Gospel Book. Right, away we go.

"Hold on! Hold on! Jonathan, will you hold the Gospel Book up in front of your face, not in front of your stomach as if you're carrying a tray of food."

They reached the front of the chapel. The acolytes and the crucifer stood aside; the sub-deacon and Jonathan entered the sanctuary and processed around the altar. The censer swung the thurible, and clouds of incense enveloped Jonathan. It took a huge effort for him not to sneeze.

"Of course, the principal as celebrant will be behind us," said the sub-deacon.

"Right, Jonathan, you will read the Gospel, and the acolytes will precede you down the aisle along with the crucifer. You will also serve the president, preparing the vessels, doing the ablutions for the president and also pronouncing the dismissal. OK?"

"Yes, sure," Jonathan replied, hoping that his lack of knowledge wouldn't be too obvious. He was going to have to look at a few Catholic eucharists on YouTube before the service began at five p.m.

The actual celebration of the Mass was, indeed, a holy mystery to Jonathan. He was mesmerised and baffled by all the hand gestures, genuflections and when to make the sign of the cross. He tried his best to keep up. Sensing his nervousness and inexperience, the principal guided him through the liturgy with gestures and whispers.

In the vestry, after the service, the principal said kindly, "Well done! That has expanded your liturgical education, I've no doubt. I'll see you in the common room after dinner and buy you a stiff drink."

Another event that filled Jonathan with dread.

***

At the community dinner, each table had bottles of white and red wine. Jonathan stuck to water. After they'd eaten, the principal welcomed students to the beginning of a new term, making special mention of Jonathan from the Church of Ireland—"our older sister across the Irish Sea." He thanked the sub-deacon for organising the Mass (loud cheers) and the chef for preparing the meal (loud cheers). Notices of college events and activities were given by some of the students. Each announcement was followed by the banging of fists on tables, and then the students and staff retired to the common room bar, where the principal sought out Jonathan.

"That was a new experience for you." He beamed broadly.

"Yes," replied Jonathan. "It seems we are a good bit lower in Dublin. A good bit lower. Some of the students don't even wear cassocks and surplices, much less the gear I was in tonight."

"We're pretty high up the candle here, though there are other places that are higher. You'll need a gin and tonic, I dare say. Then we can sit down, and you can tell me about yourself."

"Er..." Jonathan blushed. "I don't really drink. I'll have a soda and lime, if that's all right?"

"Sure. Fine," said the principal, heading off to the bar. It was a long time since he'd had a teetotaller in the college.

Chapter 4

It took a few weeks for Jonathan to become familiar with college life in Cambridge and the location of the other colleges where occasional lectures were held. He even bought a bike!

Gradually, he came to know his way around the liturgy used in the college chapel, so that when it was next his turn to be deacon at the community Mass, he was even looking forward to it. He was quietly confident that he would get everything right, even censing with the thurible.

Jonathan's next involvement in the community Mass coincided with a visit from the Bishop of Ely, who was to be president and preacher. Everything went to liturgical plan for Jonathan, and he was rather pleased with himself as he entered the common room after dinner.

The bishop sought him out, which wasn't difficult as he was the only student wearing a dog collar.

"So, you're the visiting student from Dublin?" asked the bishop as he came up to Jonathan. "Let me get you a gin and tonic and we'll find a quiet corner to have a chat.

What was Jonathan to do? Quick decision needed. He didn't want to appear as a backwoodsman from Ireland.

"Yes, that would be lovely," he heard himself say. "Thank you very much."

Was that the devil on his shoulder talking? Didn't St. Paul warn against conforming to this world? *But then*, he argued to himself, *if the bishop thinks it's all right, who am I, a mere deacon, to argue?*

He didn't have much time for theological debate with himself, as the bishop appeared at his (other) shoulder with two G&Ts and steered him to an empty couch.

"Cheers," the bishop said, taking a good mouthful.

"Cheers," said Jonathan, taking a sip. Actually, it tasted rather good. It was very refreshing, and the liquid slipped down his throat with ease. Hmm. Not at all what he expected.

"So, you've been made a deacon, but you're not yet a curate?" asked the bishop. "How does that work? Is that peculiar to the Church of Ireland, or are you a permanent deacon?"

Jonathan explained the training process adopted some years previously by the Church of Ireland, whereby ordinands were ordained as deacons in their final year of training. During that year, each deacon was placed in a training parish for three weeks out of four. For the fourth week, they returned to the institute for seminars, further study and reflection. Before they went to their curacy parishes, they are ordained as priests.

"And what do you see as the advantages of such a system?" asked the bishop.

"I think there are two," replied Jonathan. "Firstly, people in the parishes readily accept you as a deacon, as you can wear a dog collar. They see you as part of the clergy team. In placements I have done as a lay theological student, parishioners were unsure of my role and not so open as when you are ordained."

"And the other advantage?" asked the bishop.

"When you start your curacy, you're ordained a priest, and right away you're of much more use to your rector. Also, you have had a year of pastoral experience from your deacon's year."

By this time, the bishop had finished his gin and tonic and eyed his empty glass.

"Let me get you another drink," offered Jonathan. "I've been talking too much and have hardly touched mine."

"That's very kind of you," said the bishop. When Jonathan returned, the bishop was on his feet. "I mustn't keep you from the fun. I have to have a word with the principal. But thank you for the chat and the drink."

Jonathan wandered off to join a group of students he had come to know. He took a few more sips of his gin and tonic, enjoying the fresh, tangy taste, and then a larger mouthful which left him a bit light-headed—and less resolved to refuse a replacement when offered by one of his friends.

Drink in hand, he felt more incorporated into the college community and less of a stranger. Whereas before, he had regarded the goings-on with a certain amount of puritanical criticism, he now joined in their student humour and cynicism. Instead of proffering excuses for not going out to the pub for social gatherings, he now accepted their invitations.

He was beginning to enjoy himself. More surprisingly, he was coming to appreciate and enjoy the college's formal Catholic liturgy, less judgemental now than he had been. If he wasn't careful, he would soon become a Liberal Catholic!

Chapter 5

THE JONATHAN WHO was coming to the end of his placement in Cambridge was not the same apprehensive young man who timidly knocked on the door of the theological college three months previously.

The puritanical fundamentalist had morphed into a gin-drinking Liberal Catholic. Gone was the conservative insistence on cassock, surplice and black scarf, in its place a fancy for dalmatics, chasubles, albs and stoles. The once-liturgical iconoclast now had an appreciation of good liturgy, well-prepared, and preferred classical church music to catchy, repetitive choruses. Convivial nights of church gossip had replaced intense prayer groups.

Jonathan didn't want the experience to end, so before he left the college, he approached the principal to see if he might get a parish placement for six weeks before returning to be ordained priest in Daneford in September.

He would return for the end-of-year service and party in the Theological Institute in Dublin, but he would have two months to fill before pre-ordination retreat and priesting.

The principal of his adopted college agreed to see what he could do, smiling inwardly at the transformation that had taken place in Jonathan.

A day or two later, the principal called Jonathan into his office. "I have a friend in one of the northern dioceses—Liverpool—whose parish is Liberal Catholic. His curate has just finished his contractual period of three years, and he would welcome an extra pair of hands, even if just for a short while. If you give me the dates from which you would be available, I'll get my friend, Father Damien, to contact you and arrange a meeting. Let me say, it has been a pleasure for us to have you as an exchange student. I hope you have benefitted in some way from your stay."

Reluctantly, Jonathan said farewell to Cambridge and returned to Dublin for the end-of-year service and festivities. He had a brief conversation with Guy Morgan, to whom he was going as curate in September. Guy, as usual, talked about himself and the parish and never even asked about Jonathan's time in Cambridge, too busy telling him of all the opportunities he would have in St. Stephen's. Jonathan didn't interrupt, reckoning that the less Guy Morgan knew of his revised opinions the better, at this stage, anyhow.

With renewed eagerness to get back to England, Jonathan flew to Liverpool where he was met by Father Damien Woodfield, vicar of St. Agatha's in one of the leafy Liverpool suburbs.

"I've had a chat with the suffragan bishop about you doing a placement in St. Agatha's, and before she issues you with a Permission to Officiate licence, she would obviously like to meet you. She's also getting in touch with your bishop in Northern Ireland and your college principal in Dublin. I don't expect there to be any hiccups, but the procedures have to be gone through. You will also need a DBS for safeguarding purposes. Your appointment with the bishop is tomorrow morning, and I'll drive you over. It shouldn't take long. Then we'll come back to the vicarage, have some lunch and discuss your placement with us."

Jonathan was to stay in the recently vacated curate's house. Parishioners had fitted out the house with a single bed, couch and some basic kitchen utensils. It was enough to tide him over the next six weeks.

"I haven't been allocated a curate for the coming year," Damien told Jonathan as they drove from the airport. "This year's crop are all from the evangelical wing and not wanting to come to a Liberal Catholic parish. So, after you return to Dublin, we will probably rent out the house until we, hopefully, get a curate the next time round. Anyway, it's nice to have a Baldrick, even if only for six weeks."

Jonathan's puzzlement about being a 'Baldrick' must have showed, as Damien laughed and explained, "You're probably too young to have been a fan of *Blackadder*. Baldrick was his assistant."

The interview with the bishop was brief but pleasant, and Jonathan was assured that she would issue a PTO and he could start his placement in St. Agatha's.

That evening, he watched a *Blackadder* episode on YouTube. He hoped he would be a bit better—in fact, a good deal better—than Baldrick, though he was quite pleased with his own *cunning plan* to do a placement in St. Agatha's.

Chapter 6

For Jonathan, the six weeks in St. Agatha's was as good as a holiday. The congregation was warm and welcoming and well used to having curates and student placements come and go.

While the liturgy was not as choreographed or as fussy as in Cambridge services, in St. Agatha's they were both formal and relaxed, with acolytes, crucifers and lay assistants. There was a robed choir, and the music was of a high standard.

Father Damien was a good preacher, combining humour and holiness, the personal and the practical, to get his message across, and always in less than ten minutes. It was a challenge to Jonathan, who was more used to delivering a twenty- to twenty-five-minute expository sermon.

His first invitation to dinner came from the director of music and his wife, who assumed he would have a pre-prandial gin and tonic and a few glasses of wine with the meal, not to mention some port with the cheese. It was a very pleasant evening, and he wobbled rather than walked back to the curate's house in quite a euphoric state.

Indeed, drink seemed to accompany nearly every event in St. Agatha's, whether it was patronal Prosecco, Consecration Sunday cocktails, Advent aperitifs or Harvest Heinekens.

In Ireland, the pace of church life, even in busy parishes, slackened in the summer. Schools closed earlier than in England and the holiday period was longer. From mid-June to September, many congregations halved, no church meetings were held, and parish life went quiet. But in England, there was no such three-month lull. Schools closed in mid-July, and parish life continued at full tilt, only slowing a bit in August.

All of which meant that Jonathan was given plenty of opportunities to be involved in ministry of all kinds.

What surprised him was the number of funerals that Father Damien had to do. In the close-knit community of Church of Ireland parishes, all those who belonged to the parish would be well known to the rector, and he or she would be the first to be informed if there had been a death.

It seemed strange to Jonathan that in St. Agatha's, the request for a funeral often came first from the undertaker, and in many cases, the deceased had little or no church connection. As the Established Church, anyone living within the parish boundaries had a right to have a funeral conducted by the local vicar.

Similarly with weddings. Jonathan found it hard to get used to the reading of banns at services instead of getting a civil licence. As Father Damien remarked, "Banns are an anachronism. But a few years ago, General Synod voted to retain the reading of banns. It just shows how out of date the Church can be."

Father Damien made time for Jonathan apart from the more formal leadership team meetings and took him for lunch in the local pub every week as well as coffee in the vicarage.

Those six weeks flew by, and it was with a huge sense of reluctance that Jonathan prepared to return home to reconnect with his family before attending the pre-ordination retreat in Dublin.

If asked to choose between St. Stephen's, to which he was going, or St. Agatha's, which he was leaving, Jonathan would have opted for the latter.

Little did Guy Morgan realise that the Jonathan who was to become his curate was a very different person now to the person he had appointed six months previously.

Chapter 7

JONATHAN FELT NAKED as he was introduced to the St. Stephen's congregation at the main Sunday morning service after his ordination as a priest the day before. The clergy didn't wear robes at that service, and to Jonathan, it was a jarring contrast to the services in Cambridge and St. Agatha's. Everything in St. Stephen's was so informal. Instead of hymns and anthems accompanied by an organ and robed choir, there were choruses and songs led by 'a twang gang'. Six months ago, it was what had attracted him to St. Stephen's. Now, it was not to his liturgical taste.

He had to preach that morning. He thought he had got the mood right; certainly, his sermon would have gone down well in St. Agatha's, but while the congregation were complimentary at the door afterwards, Guy was not impressed.

In the vestry after the service, he said to Jonathan, "There wasn't much of a challenge in that address. It was a bit bland and liberal—and on the short side. And you could have used some visual aids to spice it up. But we'll get you there."

A bit of encouragement would have gone a long way on his first Sunday.

He had been invited to the rectory after the service. There he met Faith, Guy's wife, for the first time. Although there were only three of them, lunch was served in the large dining room. They talked a lot about their time in England, turning parishes around from poor- to well-attended. Faith was very much Guy's partner in ministry as well as in marriage and was very active in running a prayer group for women and in children's work.

They took little interest in his placements in Cambridge and Liverpool. The mention of one place or the other sparked off another set of reminiscences or stories of important people they knew. Jonathan was relieved. It would not have been wise to enthuse about either.

"Well, we mustn't detain you too long," Guy said as they finished coffee. "I'll let you get back to look over—and lengthen—your talk for tonight's youth service. It has become very popular with the young folk from all over Daneford. It is quite the place to be, and we don't want to lower the standard. Challenge them with the Gospel. And remember that after the service, there is Youth Fellowship in the hall."

"Yes, of course," Jonathan said as he stood up to go. "I look forward to it."

"You'll meet Rosie McCrea, our youth worker. We're so lucky to have her. You will be part of the team every Sunday evening. I expect my curates to work hard. Welcome to St. Stephen's."

As Jonathan walked home to his curate's house, he was perplexed within himself. St. Stephen's was very like his home parish in the North, and he had entered wholeheartedly into all that happened there, especially the youth scene. So why wasn't he bouncing with excited anticipation at the prospect of that evening's youth service and fellowship? Could six months of a different experience undo his past so much?

He was beginning to feel it could—and had!

Chapter 8

Guy Morgan and Laurence Finch, the principal of St. Olaf's School, slipped into the back seats as the youth service began.

Laurence Finch was an enthusiastic supporter of St. Stephen's and used his position in the neighbouring parish of St. Olaf's to promote St. Stephen's youth ministry, much to the annoyance of the rector of St. Olaf's, the Revd. Wendy Morris, who was also the chair of the school board of management. To say that they didn't see eye to eye would be an understatement. After Wendy had disagreed with Laurence over a few matters, she was his Enemy Number One. He loathed her as he did anyone who disagreed with him, of which there were quite a few in St. Olaf's, but they had the sense to keep quiet while their children were still in his school.

Jonathan saw them slide into the back of the church and knew he was being assessed. It didn't worry him. These kinds of services were what he was used to. He'd given many talks at such gatherings and needed no notes. He knew the formula.

Rosie McCrea led the service, and the music group played the songs. Rosie was an intriguing individual of below-average height with close-cropped blonde hair that gave her an almost boyish look. A fleur-de-lis was tattooed on each forearm and a cross on each shoulder.

Jonathan didn't have much time to talk to her that first night. After the service, she was busy with her volunteers getting the room ready for the Youth Fellowship, arranging chairs and tables, putting up the table tennis table and the snooker table and organising the tuck shop in the kitchen. Then she was mingling with the young people and talking to them.

After an hour, it all had to be put away.

As Jonathan helped her clear the room, she said, "I enjoyed your talk at the service tonight. You've obviously done this type of service before."

"And what about you?" asked Jonathan. "How long have you been the youth worker here in St. Stephen's?"

"Oh, I'm not an official, employed youth worker," laughed Rosie. "Is that what Guy Morgan told you? No, I'm a volunteer. I'm exploring ordination, and I'm on a placement here. I'm not even from Daneford, but as St. Stephen's has the reputation of being a lively church, my Dublin director of ordinands arranged with Guy for me to come here for a year. Guy likes to give the impression that he is an empire builder." She laughed again. "Actually, I'm a drama student."

She went on to explain that she had just started studying drama in university when she felt drawn to ordination. Her director of ordinands had arranged the placement in St. Stephen's to give her more time to think about it and some experience of parish life.

They talked about her course and, as they were leaving, she said that she would value a chat about his journey to ordination sometime.

Jonathan's first day was over. He was tired, but before he collapsed onto the sofa to watch some telly, he poured himself a large gin and tonic.

Chapter 9

JONATHAN THREW HIMSELF into the work of St. Stephen's, and there was always plenty to do. At the weekly staff meetings with Guy, Jonathan had to give a detailed account of how he had spent his week—which parishioners he had visited, what parish events he had attended—and Guy always had a list of other things he wanted done the following week. Guy always tried to impress Jonathan with all he, himself, did both in the parish and as archdeacon in the diocese. Nor was he short on anecdotes about how he handled difficult situations in parishes. To the clergy of Daneford, Guy Morgan was 'the oculist', the 'I Guy'.

Jonathan often came away from staff meetings feeling inadequate, despite his best efforts, and although he quickly got back into his old evangelical ways, it never really satisfied him spiritually as it once had done. He missed the liturgical order and formality he had experienced in Cambridge and St. Agatha's.

Even though his Sundays were full, he began to attend sung evensong in Daneford Cathedral some Sunday afternoons. It wasn't a service that required a lot of participation, and he found it refreshing to sit in the congregation and let it all wash over him.

He didn't want word to get back to Guy Morgan that he was attending the cathedral, so he never wore his clerical collar to the services. He always sat in the back row and slipped away before the choir and clergy recessed.

However, on one of his visits to evensong, who should he see in the congregation but Laurence Finch! Laurence spied him as he came in and beckoned to Jonathan to sit beside him. His cover was now well and truly blown! While there was no reason *not* to go to the cathedral, Jonathan knew Guy would not be pleased. In one of their conversations, he had described the cathedral as a 'museum' and its services as 'antediluvian'.

"I'm as surprised to see you here as, no doubt, you are to see me," whispered Laurence as the choir gathered at the back of the cathedral. "Let's have a cup of coffee afterwards." The choir introit began before Jonathan could reply.

Jonathan's mind was in a turmoil all through the service. He couldn't concentrate and heard little of what was said and sung.

As they passed the dean on the way out, he could see a flicker of recognition on his face as he nodded to Jonathan.

"I know you don't have a lot of time before you get back to St. Stephen's for the youth service this evening," Laurence murmured, "but there is time for a quick cup of coffee. I know a nice little café not far from here."

Full of foreboding, Jonathan sat opposite Laurence Finch as they waited for their coffee.

"I was once a choirboy in Daneford Cathedral, and every now and again, I like to attend the cathedral for old time's sake. I'm fully behind what Guy is doing in St. Stephen's. He's doing a wonderful job and has completely revitalised the parish, especially for the young folk. But I like to keep in touch with the choir even though there aren't many of my contemporaries left. And you?" he asked pointedly.

"During my last year in training, I did an exchange in a theological college in Cambridge and then a placement in an English parish. They were both quite high, and surprisingly,

I enjoyed the liturgy. So, every so often, I come to the cathedral as a sort of link with those experiences."

"Yes, I quite understand," said Laurence smoothly. "Though I'm not sure Guy would. Let's keep it a secret. He doesn't have to know. It doesn't dilute our support for St. Stephen's."

"Thank you," said Jonathan, relieved. "Now, I really must get back in time for tonight's youth service."

"Yes, you head on," said Laurence. "I'll stay for a bit and maybe meet with the choir in the pub for a post-service drink. They always get together in The Bishop's Apron opposite the cathedral after evensong."

Jonathan left with an uneasy feeling that he had been caught and was now in debt to Laurence Finch.

Chapter 10

THOUGH ONLY NINETEEN, Rosie McCrea had packed more into her short life than many would do in a lifetime.

She grew up in the suburbs of Dublin, in a large, post-war estate that was now mostly privately owned. She had a brother who was a year younger than she. Her father was a bus driver, and her mother worked part-time as a hairdresser. It was not a happy home. Rosie remembered many arguments between her parents.

Her mother suffered from severe depression, and as the years went by, she was more and more absent from work, which left the family finances depleted. The lack of money was the cause of many of the arguments. In the end, when Rosie was ten, her father left and went to live with another woman.

Rosie was a bright girl, and even though much of the running of the house and looking after her mother and younger brother fell on her, she won a scholarship to a fee-paying secondary school.

Socially, she wasn't able to keep up with the girls in her class, who were mostly from well-to-do families in the leafy suburbs of Dublin. Jealous of Rosie's academic prowess, they made snide remarks about where she came from.

Rosie was the odd girl out, bullied mercilessly by the other girls, and there wasn't a great deal of comfort or support to be had from home. Her mother was becoming more and more withdrawn and unable to do even the most basic of chores. While Rosie's dad contacted her from time to time and gave her some pocket money, he had started a new family with his partner, so there was little chance of him returning home.

Rosie did make friends with one of the girls in her class. Chloe was also on the edges, being far too quiet and serious for the in-group of their year. It was through Chloe that Rosie started going to church.

Immanuel was not your average Church of Ireland church. It had started as a multi-denominational house group and had quickly grown; needing somewhere bigger to meet, they hired the assembly hall of a school nearby.

An ailing congregation in one of the inner-city churches was facing closure, and the leaders of Immanuel approached the Church of Ireland authorities to take over the church.

Protracted negotiations took place between Immanuel and the Church Councils. In the end, it was agreed they could take over the church provided that, however loosely, they became part of the structure of the Church of Ireland and an ordained chaplain, appointed by the archbishop, became their leader. The existing congregation would be provided with a liturgical service every Sunday.

Immanuel Church continued to grow and became the envy of many other churches in Dublin, as its lively and informal worship attracted many evangelicals in outlying parishes as well as students from colleges and universities in Dublin.

Immanuel proved a lifeline for Rosie. She was accepted and welcomed by the congregation. She found a faith she never knew she had and friends who were genuinely interested in her. Immanuel was an anchor in the rather stormy seas of home and school life.

She was baptised by total immersion in the new coffin-shaped pool that had been built beneath the floor at the back of the church. It was, according to the chaplain, Bob, to show that baptism was a real dying to sin and rising to new life.

Then disaster struck. Her mother took an overdose, which killed her. The people at Immanuel were totally supportive of Rosie and her brother, enfolding them literally and metaphorically in loving arms. Bob took care of the funeral arrangements, and Immanuel was full of caring people on the day her mother was laid to rest.

Rosie went to live with her grandparents while her brother was taken in by an aunt and uncle.

It all happened during Rosie's last year in school, but she did well enough in her exams to win a place in college studying drama.

She had reconnected with her father after the funeral, and he had promised to help with her fees. Decisions had yet to be made about the family home, but in the meantime, she continued to live with her grandparents, who gave her much love and support.

In the upheaval of her life, she felt a call to be ordained. She discussed it with Bob, who put her in touch with the diocesan director of ordinands. He wanted her to take her time and test her sense of vocation for a while longer to make sure it wasn't merely something that gave her a sense of security at an unsettling time.

Chapter 11

"YOU'D BETTER PUT in an appearance at the Clerical next Thursday," ordered Guy as he and Jonathan met for their weekly staff meeting.

"What's a Clerical? asked Jonathan, confused.

As if to a stupid child, Guy Morgan replied, "The Clerical is the monthly meeting of clergy in an area, hosted by one of them, which includes a lunch followed by a paper. I'm sure you know what a paper is."

Jonathan said nothing.

"I've a senior team meeting with the bishop, so thankfully, I will not be there. But it will be good for St. Stephen's to be represented, and it will also be an opportunity for you to meet the local clergy. Next Thursday's is at…" He fiddled with his phone. "St. Olaf's."

"That's Wendy Morris's parish, isn't it?" asked Jonathan.

"And let me give you a word of warning about that lady," Guy said grimly. "She's not all sweetness and light, though she likes to give that impression. She has a nasty, vindictive streak and is too independent-minded for my liking. She refused even to countenance the imaginative reordering of churches in Lislea I proposed.

"Laurence Finch is the unfortunate principal of St. Olaf's, and he has told me of all that he has to put up with from her as chairperson of the school board of management. Laurence, as you must know by now, is a good guy, very supportive of me and of St. Stephen's. Yet with all his experience, she seems to delight in challenging him on how to run his school. He even had to get the teachers' union to restrain her from meddling and put her in her place.

"And then there was that fishy business when her organist was shot leaving her rectory late one night—when his wife was away. Not very proper, if you ask me. All sorts of inferences could be made. You watch yourself around her. The bishop is fond of her, but he doesn't know her like I do.

"Now to the rest of the week..."

As Jonathan left the rectory, he realised that it didn't do to get on the wrong side of the archdeacon or to fall out with Laurence Finch. Guy Morgan obviously didn't know about Laurence's visits to the cathedral, or about his own. He would have to be careful and look up who was preaching at evensong in case it might be the archdeacon.

Jonathan attended the Clerical that Thursday. A lunch of soup and sandwiches was served from noon to one p.m., during which the clergy mingled and chatted. Wendy welcomed Jonathan after she had said grace. He felt very much the new boy, but they all seemed friendly enough and welcomed him to the area.

Wendy introduced herself to Jonathan and told him that they were neighbours and introduced him to Steve Adams—"another new boy to Lislea" and rector of St. Saviour's on the outskirts of the town.

They chatted about this and that, and she seemed genuinely interested in him and in his time in England, promising to keep in touch.

"Ah, now I can put a name to the face that appeared in the cathedral last Sunday." A cleric, a few years older than Jonathan, came over to talk to him. "I'm Daniel Norton, dean's vicar at the cathedral. We don't usually get many from St. Stephen's at evensong," he laughed, "but you are most welcome. I heard that you did a term in Cambridge. Don't be surprised.

I hear all the gossip. St. Stephen's is not noted for its excellence in Anglican liturgy, so do please come again. And maybe when you have a Sunday evening off, you might join myself and the choir for a few drinks in The Bishop's Apron across from the cathedral. It's always a jolly time. Sorry I can't stay," said Daniel with a wink. "Duty calls but think about that invitation." With that, he left.

They were called into the sitting room for the paper—on Melchizedek in the Letter to the Hebrews—which was being given by one of the retired clergy, a former lecturer in a theological college.

Heads began to nod, yawns were stifled, and there were a few unstifled snores. There was no discussion after the paper, and the meeting ended rather abruptly. Jonathan was back in his house by two-fifteen p.m.!

Chapter 12

Jonathan left it a few weeks before he went to evensong in the cathedral again. He didn't want to bump into Laurence Finch. He waited until the service had started, scanned the congregation from the back of the cathedral to make sure there was no Finch and then took a seat and let the service work its magic for his soul.

While not denying his evangelical roots, he felt as if had matured into the Liberal Catholic ethos. He tried to put a finger on what attracted him, apart from the liturgy, and concluded that Liberal Catholicism was broader and more inclusive than the rather narrow and judgmental attitude of many evangelicals.

The dean's vicar, Daniel Norton, greeted him warmly as he left the cathedral. "I'm sure you have an evening service or something, but don't forget that invitation for a few drinks is always there. The choir may look sober and solemn in the stalls, but they're good company and you'll enjoy them."

"Yes, I'll keep it in mind," replied Jonathan. "I have a week off coming soon, and that might be a plan."

He hurried off to check over his talk for the youth service. Rosie had again mentioned having a chat about ordination, and he had invited her round to the curate's house after the Youth Fellowship.

His house was a little three-bedroom semi a few streets away from the church. The ground floor consisted of a kitchen/diner and a sitting room. Jonathan used one of the bedrooms as a study. The smallest was a guest room. He seldom had people to stay, and when his parents visited, he gave them his double room and used the single room himself.

He showed Rosie into the kitchen, and she sat at the dining table as he made two cups of coffee.

"Your talks at the youth services are really good," Rosie said. "They remind me of the services we have in Immanuel."

"I don't think I have heard of Immanuel. Where is it?"

"In Dublin, not far from the city centre. It started as a prayer group but then took over a city church that was going to close. It's quite charismatic and very lively. I don't think the archbishop is completely at home when he visits." She laughed.

"So, it's part of the Church of Ireland?" asked Jonathan.

"Sort of. We can send representatives to the Diocesan Synod. The archdeacon comes from time to time to see that we are behaving." She laughed again. "But we have quite a whack of money to pay to the diocese for the privilege, and we have to pay for all repairs and running costs. I suppose the diocese does pay for the chaplain, Bob," she conceded.

"And were you a member of the original congregation at that church?"

"Oh, gosh, no!" Rosie replied. "I never grew up in any kind of church. My parents didn't bother with religion. My father left us when I was nine, and looking after my mother, who was never well, and my brother took all my time. Anyway, what church would welcome such a poor, dysfunctional family like mine? At least, that's what I thought at the time."

Rosie went on to tell Jonathan about being bullied at school and how her one and only friend, Chloe, introduced her to Immanuel, where she was accepted.

"How is your mother now?" asked Jonathan.

"I'm afraid she took her own life last year. She was due to be taken into a care home. The prospect terrified her, and she took the only course she knew to prevent it. She would have been sectioned if she'd refused."

Rosie's upbringing was such a contrast to Jonathan's, and he began to realise what a safe, sheltered childhood he'd had.

"And ordination?" he asked.

"The strange thing is that in the middle of all that was happening, I felt God was putting it into my head to be ordained. I had a chat with Bob, our chaplain in Immanuel, and he put me in touch with the cleric who looks after vocations. I suppose he felt that it might all be just a flash-in-the-pan reaction to my mother's suicide, and he arranged for me to spend time here in St. Stephen's before taking it further."

She paused, looked Jonathan in the eye, and said, "And that's Rosie McCrea, warts 'n' all."

She looked at her phone. "Heck, I'd better be going or I'll miss the last bus to Dublin. Perhaps we can continue this chat sometime?"

"Sure," replied Jonathan as Rosie collected her coat and headed for the door.

She was rather disappointed that he hadn't offered her a lift home.

Chapter 13

Ellie Jones lived with her two children, Mia and Noah, in a cul-de-sac in one of Lislea's new estates. Mia was eleven and Noah was ten. Ellie's husband, Ollie, had died two years previously while playing rugby for Lislea.

Ollie had been a fit thirty-five-year-old and had always seemed healthy. Ellie had been nagging him for some time to give up playing rugby as he wasn't that young anymore, but Ollie loved the sport and had continued to tog out for the team every week. His death was totally unexpected and had been put down to 'sudden death syndrome'.

His death had thrown Ellie's life into turmoil. Although Ollie had life insurance, it wasn't enough to pay off their mortgage, and with two young children, their savings were meagre.

Ollie and Elie had been childhood sweethearts, having met when they were in secondary school. Their romance continued after they left school and survived university; they had married shortly after they had both graduated. They even had jobs in the same bank—Ollie in IT, Ellie in finance. After Ollie's death, Ellie negotiated part-time hours—the bank had been surprisingly sympathetic—so that she could be at home when Mia and Noah finished school. Her mother and father lived only a few miles away and did all they could to help, but her father had been diagnosed with cancer and her mother wasn't as available as she would like to be.

The Joneses were members of St. Stephen's, and Guy Morgan had been a great support at the time of Ollie's death and continued to keep in touch with Ellie.

"And have you thought of where Mia might go to school after finishing in St. Stephen's?" he asked one day when he had dropped in to see how they were doing.

"Ollie and I always wanted Mia and Noah to go to our old school. I could drop them off on the way to work and collect them afterwards. But on my salary, the fees are prohibitive. The only chance would be a scholarship for Mia. She's bright, but maybe not bright enough to win a scholarship."

Guy thought for a moment. "You know Laurence Finch, the principal of St. Olaf's. He's a really good guy and one of our main people here in St. Stephen's. Maybe he could prepare Mia for the scholarship exam. Let me put out feelers and see what his response might be."

And so it was that after school once a week, Laurence Finch would stop by at the Joneses' house and give Mia extra tuition to help her prepare for the scholarship exam. Ellie was always there to let him in, and to keep the house quiet, Noah would go to play with his pal next door, whose father, Declan, worked from home and was always there to supervise.

Though they were both parishioners of St. Stephen's, Ellie couldn't say that she knew Laurence Finch well, but as she got to know him, she found him charming and helpful and patient with Mia. He was nearly becoming one of the family.

Chapter 14

What struck Jonathan Appleford about ministry as he finished his first year in St. Stephen's was the relentless nature of the job.

Guy Morgan was like a Duracell bunny. He never seemed to stop. He was always on the go attending to parish and diocesan duties, and he expected Jonathan to follow his example of constant busy-ness.

Most days, Jonathan had very little time to himself, and when it came to his day off, he was usually so exhausted that he stayed in bed most of the morning, did housework and shopping in the afternoon and lounged in front of the telly in the evening with a takeaway, a bottle of wine and a few gin and tonics.

Saturday was his day off, and often he would have a bit of a hangover on Sunday morning, especially when he was taking the early morning communion service.

He used to play rugby in school and in university. Lislea had a rugby team and was always on the lookout for new players. He could have played on one of the lower teams on Saturdays but, he convinced himself, he hadn't time to go training and anyway, he was too tired after a busy week trying to keep up with all that his rector gave him to do. He did go jogging every so often but found it lonely and boring.

The result was that while he knew a lot of people, he had no real friends, male or female, though a lot of girls in the parish had their eyes on him. Getting into a relationship with a girl from the parish would be easy, but he realised, it might not be as easy to get out of it.

And then there was Rosie McCrea. He couldn't make up his mind about her. She was good-looking, she was fun and she had faith, but as he mulled over what she had told him about her broken family, he couldn't overcome his innate caution and, he had to admit, a certain snobbery. What would his straitlaced, evangelical, middle-class parents make of Rosie?

He decided that he must make contact with Daniel Norton, the dean's vicar in the cathedral. He reminded Jonathan of many of the theological students he had got to know in Cambridge.

He had a week off coming up. He had planned to visit his parents in the North, but maybe, instead of setting off on the Saturday, he would leave it until the Monday. That would mean he could go to evensong on the Sunday, go with Daniel for a few drinks with the choir afterwards in The Bishop's Apron.

Yes, that was a plan. And it cheered him up no end.

Chapter 15

"It's all working out so well," Ellie Jones told Guy Morgan after church one Sunday morning. "Laurence Finch calls once a week on his way home from St. Olaf's. He and Mia seem to have hit it off really well. I'm back from the office just before the children come home from school and have time to make Laurence a cup of tea before he starts his lesson with Mia."

"He's a fine person," said Guy. "If anyone can help Mia with getting a scholarship, it's Laurence."

Before leaving the Joneses' house one evening shortly after Ellie had spoken to Guy, Laurence Finch said to Ellie, "Mia's coming along so well. She's applying herself to the work I give her and is making really good progress. I'd like to give her some reward, to encourage her to keep on working hard. How about I bring the three of you to the cinema tomorrow night? There's a rerun of *Shaun the Sheep* at the Odeon. It's at six-thirty, and we could all go to McDonald's afterwards. If that's not too childish a night out for you."

"What a pity I can't go. I have a meeting of the St. Stephen's Women's Group. As I'm on the committee, I suppose I had better be there, but the children would have loved that."

"Maybe some other time then? Unless..." Laurence paused. "If you're OK with it, I can take Mia and Noah myself and have them back by nine-thirty, by which time you will be back from the women's group. It's just that Mia is doing so well, I'd like to reward her in a practical way."

Ellie had no objection, and so, after Mia's tuition session with Laurence Finch the following week, Mia and Noah piled into the back seat of Laurence Finch's car and headed to the Odeon in Lislea.

On arrival at the cinema, he treated the children to popcorn and minerals, and afterwards, as promised, he took them to McDonald's where they were allowed to order whatever they chose.

Mia was getting to know Laurence Finch well and chatted away to him. As Noah was next door with Joel and his dad during Mia's tuition sessions, he didn't know him well, and anyway, Mr. Finch was a teacher and to be treated with caution as far as Noah was concerned. Noah was often in trouble for bad behaviour at school, and teachers were definitely not among his favourite adults, but Joel's dad didn't seem to think much of Mr. Finch either.

Ellie greeted them at the front door. "Mia and Noah, it's time you went to bed. Say thank you to Mr. Finch for a lovely evening."

Having said their thanks, they headed upstairs. Laurence made to go, but Ellie said, "Would you like a coffee or a drink? I'm really grateful for all that you're doing for Mia."

"Well, if it's not too late for you, that would be very nice. Something to wash away the lingering taste of McDonald's fine dining."

"There's a bottle of red wine open. Would you like a glass? I'm sure one drink won't put you over the limit."

"Well, just one," laughed Laurence.

Ellie showed him into their comfortable living room. Photos of Ollie, and of Ollie and Ellie and their two children, hung on the walls and rested on the mantelpiece over the fireplace.

Laurence asked about Ollie, and Ellie told him the story of his sudden death. She felt comforted by sharing again how their happiness had been shattered by what had happened.

Laurence looked at his watch. "Well, I'm afraid I must be going. I still have a few things to get ready for school tomorrow. Thank you for the wine."

"No, thank you for giving Mia and Noah such an enjoyable evening, and thank you for all you're doing for Mia, and for being such a good listener."

Chapter 16

Jonathan's week off at last. No sermon to prepare. No talk for the youth service. No responsibilities for a week. A chance to go to both services in the cathedral and to have a few drinks with Daniel Norton and the choir after evensong.

Jonathan checked the cathedral website just to make sure that Guy Morgan wasn't preaching—it would be just his luck if he was—but he wasn't.

Sunday morning, Jonathan lay in bed listening to the bells of St. Stephen's calling the faithful to the early morning communion. And he didn't have to go. Bliss!

After a leisurely breakfast, he set off for the Eucharist in the cathedral, which, he was surprised to note, was very well-attended. Maybe there were more people in Lislea who liked a well-done traditional liturgy than Guy Morgan would have liked to admit. Sitting in the cathedral, Jonathan closed his eyes and imagined himself back in Cambridge.

At the door after the service, Daniel Norton made a beeline for him. "Ah, this must be your Sunday off. Are you free to join us for a drink after evensong? I'd like to offer to buy you lunch, but I'm already committed to joining the dean and this morning's preacher. But look forward to seeing you later."

"That's all right," Jonathan replied. "I've already booked myself in at that new bistro in the town centre. It's been getting a lot of good reviews. I'll let you know what it's like."

Jonathan bought the *Sunday Times*, ordered a half-bottle of wine and browsed through the paper as he waited for his meal.

So this is how the majority spend their Sundays, he thought. Not bad!

After lunch, he looked around the Lislea Book Shop and then made his way to the cathedral and was relieved that there was no sign of Laurence Finch in the congregation.

Once again, evensong washed over him, the music doing far more for him spiritually than the shallow choruses of the youth service loudly led by St. Stephen's music group.

"Come back to the chapter room while I get out of this gear," said Daniel after the service. "Then we'll head over to The Bishop's Apron to join the choir."

The choir had their own section of the pub reserved for them every Sunday evening, and there was plenty of talk and laughter coming from their direction.

"Now what can I get you to drink? Then I'll introduce you to the group."

"A gin and tonic would be great," replied Jonathan with an ease that would have shocked him a few years ago.

Drinks in hand, Daniel stepped into the centre of the gathering. "Ladies and gentlemen, I'd like to introduce you to one of our secret admirers, the Reverend Jonathan Appleford, priest at that bastion of high Anglicanism, St. Stephen's, Lislea, and curate assistant of our beloved and esteemed archdeacon, the Venerable Guy Morgan."

There was a cheer from the choir and a clinking of glasses. Two of the younger male members pulled up an empty chair for Jonathan to join them.

"Welcome to our liquid version of vespers. I'm Nigel and this is Patrick. Now tell us about yourself and how someone from Lislea's citadel of evangelicalism has started coming to the cathedral."

"Although he's not the only one," added Patrick. "Doesn't Laurence Finch also hail from St. Stephen's?"

"Oh, him!" retorted Nigel. "He's a funny fish. Always wants to be in with our group yet never really fitting. Almost as if he's putting up a false front to hide his real self."

"Well, he's the archdeacon's right-hand man," said Jonathan. "Guy Morgan thinks the world of him. I saw him at the cathedral once, and he said he used to sing in the choir and likes to keep up the link."

"He gives me the creeps," shuddered Nigel. "But look, we're not here to talk about Finch, but about you, Jonathan. So, tell us all about yourself. Surely, a good-looking specimen like you has a girlfriend, or maybe a boyfriend?" He raised his eyebrows and looked straight at Jonathan.

Jonathan blushed. "Neither."

"Oh, we'll have to see about that, won't we, Patrick? Order that hunk another drink, will you?"

Jonathan lost count of the drinks with which he was plied, and feeling more than a bit light-headed and dizzy, he decided to get a taxi home. He didn't trust himself to get on the right bus, but he was happy. He'd had a very sociable and enjoyable evening, and he promised himself he would do it again—soon.

Chapter 17

"WE MISSED YOU last Sunday night." said Rosie as they were clearing up after Youth Fellowship the following Sunday evening. "Especially as I had to do the talk, which was not up to your standard, I have to confess." She laughed. "But I would still like to have a chat with you about ordination," she said, suddenly serious. "Have you time for a cup of coffee when we're done, or is there another time that would suit?"

"Er, um, I have a lot of catching up to do this week, what with having time off. Guy makes no allowances, as you know. But, yes, why not? Come back to my place—though I'll have to go to the corner shop on the way to get some milk. I'm afraid that the fridge is empty having been away. But I do have scones and cakes that my mum sent me back with."

Back in the kitchen of the curate's house, Jonathan put on the kettle, got out some cups and opened a plastic container full of homemade biscuits.

They sat at the kitchen table. "Now where do you want to start?" asked Jonathan.

"Well, I mean, what type of person are they looking for at the Selection Conference? I don't know whether I would fit in."

"The main thing the selectors are looking for is a genuine sense of vocation—that you believe God is calling you to be ordained—and that it has been recognised by others who know you. They look at areas like leadership potential, your understanding of the Church of Ireland, your involvement in the life and work of the Church, how you relate to people, and so on."

"But I'm a relative newcomer to the Church of Ireland, and to faith," Rosie admitted, adding, "and my family life has been a bit…chaotic, to say the least. That's why I wonder if I would fit in." She frowned and looked down at her hands.

"Oh, don't worry about that." Jonathan laughed. "Clergy are a real ragbag of personalities and backgrounds. There was a time, long ago now, when clergy were all a bit monochrome, but not anymore. Even in the Church of Ireland. When I was in Cambridge, I even came across transgender ordinands, and there were plenty of gay students. I must say, at first, it was all a bit of an eye-opener for me, and to be honest, with my background, I found it hard to accept. But it made me a lot more open-minded and accepting of difference."

"I'm not gay or anything like that," said Rosie, reddening. "What I mean is that if they look into my background, they will find a lot of dysfunction."

"I think the really important thing they will be looking for is how you have dealt with all you have experienced, not with the situation itself. Have you come to terms with it? Is it still pressing buttons in your life? That sort of thing."

"I think I have. The people in Immanuel have been really helpful and supportive and have prayed me through all that has happened."

"There will be a psychologist on the panel," Jonathan went on, "but you seem to me to be a well-adjusted person. So don't worry."

"Thank you," replied Rosie. "I really appreciate all of that." She stretched out across the table to take Jonathan's hand.

Was it a gesture of thanks for listening or a timid advance? Jonathan didn't know and didn't withdraw his hand.

With a slight blush, she took her hand away. "Tell me more about your time in England. It sounds as if you had a really interesting time."

In the evangelical climate of St. Stephen's, there weren't many with whom Jonathan could share his experiences in Cambridge and Liverpool. He was glad of the opportunity to talk to Rosie about them.

And she was a good listener. It was very late when Jonathan finished telling her of the people and the different ways of doing things he had found in his five months in the Church of England.

Rosie looked at her phone. "Gosh, I've missed the last bus. I'd better ring for a taxi."

"Not at all, my fault for rabbiting on. I'll give you a lift home."

When they reached her grandparents' house, she said, "Thank you for this evening," and put her hand on his arm, pausing for a long moment before she opened the passenger door and headed into the house.

Chapter 18

"I'M AFRAID I overbought for supper tonight," said Ellie Jones as she came into the lounge near the end of Laurence Finch's tuition session with Mia. "There will be more than enough for four of us if you'd care to stay for something to eat? It will be something simple, not cordon bleu." She laughed.

"As it happens, I don't have any arrangements for this evening. And I'd be going home to rustle up a meal for myself, so thank you very much. I'd love to!"

So it became rather a ritual that on Thursday evening, after his teaching session with Mia, Laurence would stay for something to eat with the Joneses. He never outstayed his welcome, though Ellie would not have minded if he had stayed on for a chat. Laurence could be good company and could put on the charm when he chose to.

"Don't want the neighbours talking," he'd say with a laugh as he left their house.

"He's a really nice man, isn't he?" Ellie said to the children one evening when she came into the lounge after Laurence Finch had gone home.

"He's OK," said Mia, noncommittally.

"I don't like him," Noah said defiantly. "He's too nice at times—for a teacher."

"Oh, come on, Noah, you hardly know him, and he's a great help to Mia. We should be grateful to him for all he's doing to prepare her for the scholarship exam. Maybe he will help you one day."

"Never!" declared Noah as he stomped off to his room to do his homework.

***

It was the evening of the last teaching session before Mia would sit for the scholarship Saturday week, as it was half-term and Laurence Finch was away on holiday. That would give Mia ten days for revision of all they had covered.

Ellie was driving home to be with the children and to let Laurence Finch in. Her mind was not on her driving but thinking about the upcoming exam. Thus, she didn't notice the traffic lights had turned amber and suddenly saw the red light. She hit the brake pedal. There was a thud as the car behind her drove into her. She was catapulted forward and then enveloped by the air bag, which saved her from hitting the windscreen.

Cars started honking their horns when the lights turned green, their drivers not realising what had happened.

An elderly man appeared at the car window. Ellie opened the door. "I hope you're not injured," he said, concern and worry written all over his face. "I was too close to you. Pull over to the side of the road and we'll look at the damage. I take full responsibility and will pay for any repairs."

"But I have to get home to let the children in from school, and my daughter is having a final tuition session," wailed Ellie.

"It shouldn't take too long to exchange names and addresses and insurance details. And we'd better report this to the police," the old man said. "We'd better do this properly."

Knowing that Mia had a key for the house for emergencies like this, Ellie rang her. "I'm going to be a little late. Someone has run into the back of my car. Will you let Mr. Finch in and tell him what's happened. I'll be there as soon as I can."

It took over an hour for the police to arrive. They inspected the damage, took statements and urged Ellie to wait for an ambulance to check she was all right. She was in considerable pain across her shoulders and chest from where the seat belt had restrained her, but she wasn't seriously injured and, luckily, her car was driveable with only a big dent in the boot.

She arrived home as Laurence Finch was leaving her house. He seemed to be in a bit of a hurry.

"I'm sorry for the delay. I hope Mia explained what happened. I'm afraid I have nothing prepared for supper."

"That's the least of your worries after all that has happened," Laurence said kindly. "But as it is, I cannot stay this evening. I have to be away. I think I've covered everything for Mia to sit the exam on Saturday."

"I can't thank you enough, Laurence. You've been such a help."

When Laurence got into his car, Mia rushed out of the house and threw her arms around Ellie, crying, "Mummy, Mummy!"

"There, there. Everything's OK. I'm all right. It's only the car that got bumped, and that can be fixed."

Noah stood in the doorway, looking sullen and angry. "I hate that Mr. Finch," he snarled.

"Leave it for now, Noah, please!" said Ellie. "Look, let me go and get changed and compose myself and we'll go to Macdonald's for supper this evening. It'll do us all good."

"But Mummy..." started Mia.

Ellie, frazzled after the accident, cut across her. "Not now, Mia, please. Everything will be sorted. Just leave it for the moment."

In her own upset, Ellie didn't notice Mia's distress.

Chapter 19

MIA'S BEHAVIOUR OVER the following few days baffled Ellie. The night of Ellie's accident, Mia had wet the bed, and she had become withdrawn. When Ellie asked her if anything was bothering her, Mia would fly into a rage and stomp off to her room. When Ellie tried to cuddle her, she would stiffen and didn't respond.

With the scholarship exam just days away, Ellie put Mia's behaviour down to anxiety. Laurence Finch had assured Ellie that Mia was bright enough and had a very good chance of winning a scholarship, but her present behaviour was puzzling and didn't bode well for sitting the exam.

Ellie tried to get Mia to talk about what was worrying her.

"You wouldn't understand!" Mia shouted and left the room.

As trying to get Mia to talk about what was upsetting her only seemed to make matters worse, Ellie said nothing and focused on creating a calm atmosphere until the scholarship exam was over.

On Saturday morning, Ellie had difficulty persuading Mia to get up. At last, she appeared for breakfast tired and listless. Ellie noticed that Mia's bed was wet yet again.

"I don't want to do this stupid exam. I don't care where I go to school. It's not important!" Mia declared angrily.

"Give it a try," soothed Ellie. "Mr Finch thinks you will fly through it."

"What does he care?" snapped Mia.

Ellie said nothing but wondered what had happened to her sweet, bright, enthusiastic daughter.

Ellie drove a very reluctant child to sit the exam at the school that she and Ollie had attended. It brought back so many happy memories, but Ellie knew Mia's heart was not in doing the exam and that she would have to look at alternative schools.

That Saturday evening, Ellie had organised for the three of them to go out for a meal to mark the end of Mia's extra classes and the completion of the scholarship exam. Instead of the happy occasion she had envisaged, it was dismal. Mia and Noah sat defiantly silent. Noah ate his food, but Mia picked at her plate and played with her iPhone. There was no chat about school or scholarship—or anything.

Ellie fumed inside but knew that a cross word would only make things worse. She needed to get to the bottom of Mia's change of character and behaviour, and that evening, she went to Mia's bedroom and sat on the bed.

"Mia, what happened that upset you so much? It isn't just the exam this morning, is it? You seemed so confident about it over the last few weeks. Has anything else occurred—in school, with your friends? Has Noah been a pest?"

Mia turned her head away and faced the wall.

"Mia, I'm your mum. I love you and we've been pals and supported each other since Dad died. You're too important to me. I just want to be able to help you. What's wrong, sweetheart?"

"He tried to kiss me…and put his hand…where…where he shouldn't," sobbed Mia, turning to Ellie and throwing her arms around her neck.

"Who?" asked Ellie. "Who did that?"

Tears rolled down Mia's cheeks. "Mr. Finch."

"What? But…I was always in the house."

"It was at the last session. There was no one here. It was horrible." Mia pulled away and rolled into a foetal position.

"That Thursday. The day I had the accident and was so late home. Oh God!" It was Ellie's turn to burst into tears and be comforted by Mia. "I'm so sorry. I let you down. I should've been here!"

Mother and daughter clung to each other. "Did he do anything else?" asked Ellie fearfully.

"No. As soon as he started, I ran out of the room and locked myself in my bedroom. Then I heard him go out the front door."

"Did he try anything before that?" asked Ellie anxiously.

"No! But he did move his chair closer to mine and tried to be sort of friendly, leaning over my books. I could smell his breath. It was horrible!"

"So it was only on that last day that he actually touched you?"

"Yes. And then you arrived home."

No wonder he'd been in such a hurry to get away.

Chapter 20

MIA SEEMED TO return more to her former self after she'd told Ellie what had happened with Laurence Finch. While it was a relief to see Mia less sulky and aggressive, Ellie was boiling with anger inside and determined that a first step would be to talk with Guy Morgan, her rector, who had recommended Laurence Finch to give tuition to Mia.

She didn't say over the phone why she wanted to see Guy, and it took a few days before an appointment could be arranged. Guy was caught up in diocesan meetings. He thought Ellie just wanted to say thanks for his help and didn't prioritise her request.

Guy showed Ellie into his study. He was all smiles and at his best-affable self. He didn't sense Ellie's pent-up fury.

"A cup of coffee?" he asked.

"No, thank you. This isn't a social call," replied Ellie coldly.

"Oh, well, take a seat." Guy indicated an armchair. "What's on your mind?"

"That man, Laurence Finch, whom you recommended to teach Mia after school. That's *who* is on my mind."

"Oh, yes, I was going to ask you how that went. The scholarship exams were last Saturday, weren't they? I do hope Mia will be successful."

"I very much doubt it," retorted Ellie. "Not after what that monster did to my daughter!"

"I don't understand what you're saying. I have the highest regard for Mr. Finch and all he does, as a teacher and as a member of St. Stephen's."

"Including molesting young girls?" Ellie shot back.

"What?!" Guy composed himself. "You must surely have got this all wrong! I can't believe this of Laurence Finch."

"Two weeks ago, I had a car accident. I was on my way home when Laurence Finch was tutoring Mia, but the police were called to the accident, and it all took some time. I only arrived as…that man was leaving. And he was in a hurry and flustered."

"Perhaps he had another engagement and was running late," countered Guy.

"I doubt that," replied Ellie. "What I have no doubt about is that he behaved inappropriately with Mia. He tried to kiss her and touch her private parts. And she, a twelve-year old girl! That's child abuse!"

"Come now, Mrs. Jones, that's a very serious accusation to make. How can you be sure that is what happened?"

"Because my daughter told me. And because of the state of mind he left her in."

"But Mia is at an impressionable age. And, what with all they see on social media—I hadn't realised until recently that it's so horrific. Don't you think that Mia was just imagining it?" asked Guy in his most syrupy, pastoral voice.

"Does that explain her bed-wetting? Something she has never done since she was a baby. Does that explain her mood swings over the last number of days?" Ellie was seething.

"I have a daughter of that age myself. Twelve is a difficult age for young girls. Hormones are flying all over the place. Their moods change by the hour. You never know where you are with them, and they probably don't know themselves. Anyway, I have only the highest regard for Mr. Finch's integrity. You say that he tried to kiss and touch Mia. Did anything physical actually happen?"

"I don't think so, no. Mia immediately got up from the table and ran from the room. Noah was outside and heard her screaming."

"So, nothing really happened. It's only Mia's word, the word of an impressionable twelve-year old, against the word of a highly respected headteacher who was only doing you a favour. I hardly think that will stand." Guy sat back and smiled. QED. Case dismissed.

"I would have thought that with all that has gone on in churches, you would, at least, have taken this more seriously," snapped Ellie, getting out of her seat. "You will obviously defend that horrible man against my vulnerable child. You disgust me as much as your precious Laurence Finch."

She made for the door.

"There is no absolute proof," Guy replied defensively. "Would you wreck a good man's reputation, and indeed the reputation of St. Stephen's, over unsubstantiated evidence?"

"You are defending the institution rather than the victim. Please let me out! You will never see me or any member of my family in St. Stephen's again. I expected better. How could I have been so wrong? On second thoughts, I'll let myself out!"

Ellie walked out defiantly, but as soon as she got into her car, she dissolved in tears.

Chapter 21

"I'VE BEEN GIVEN two tickets for a play in Dublin. We're studying it as part of our drama course. I wondered if you'd like to come along with me?"

Jonathan and Rosie were clearing up after the Sunday night Youth Fellowship meeting.

"When is it?" asked Jonathan.

"It's next Friday evening. I know Friday isn't your day off, but I didn't see any meetings scheduled in the parish diary for that evening. So I thought you might be free." She tried to keep a defiant tone out of her suggestion. "But see how you are fixed."

"That's very kind of you. No, I've nothing planned. So, yes, that should be OK, thanks." Jonathan had detected a certain challenge in her invitation.

In truth, he wasn't sold on the idea of going on a date, as that was clearly how Rosie saw it, but he had to work with her and he didn't want bad feelings between them. "I look forward to it," he added.

They arranged where to meet and at what time.

"I'm afraid I've got to rush off tonight. I have a school assembly in the morning, and I haven't a clue what I'm going to say." He didn't want it to become a habit that they went back to his place every Sunday evening. He still wasn't sure about her.

On the way back to his house, he reflected that maybe he had been too quick to accept Rosie's invitation for the following Friday. He knew she would like a romantic relationship to develop between them. But…what would his parents make of her with her cropped hair and tattoos? Not much, he knew. And if they found out about her family history, they would not be impressed and would try to get him to put an end to their relationship.

He was torn. Rosie was good company, different to any of the girls he had gone out with before, who were rather prim and proper. But would he want his parents to meet her?

He was losing his evangelical certainty not only in matters of faith but also of the heart.

Friday night came and they met in an Italian restaurant for something to eat before the theatre.

The play itself was very modern and chaotic and way over Jonathan's head. Rosie seemed immersed in it, with a clear appreciation of what was going on.

They went to a nearby bar afterwards where, sensing his incomprehension, she explained to Jonathan what the play was all about. They had a few drinks and the conversation flowed easily between them.

It was Jonathan's turn to say that he had better go or he would miss the last bus. Rosie said that her grandparents didn't live too far away and that she would walk home. She assured Jonathan that she often did so. It was along main streets and there would be no danger.

Apart from not understanding the play, Jonathan had enjoyed the evening. It made a change from the usual lonely Friday evening in front of the telly.

It made him realise that he needed to cultivate some friendships and to keep up contact with Daniel Norton and the members of the cathedral choir.

Chapter 22

Hidden amongst a pile of junk mail on the hall carpet awaiting Ellie's return from work was an envelope with Ellie's old school crest. It was just like the envelopes that used to contain her school reports back in the day.

The scholarship results. She remembered the feelings of dread when her school reports dropped through the letterbox. They came flooding back as she took up the envelope.

She made a cup of coffee first and then sat down at the kitchen table and slit the letter open.

> *Dear Mrs. Jones,*
>
> *I regret to tell you that your daughter, Mia, has not been successful in being awarded a scholarship to our school. She did well in the examination but, unfortunately, did not attain a sufficiently high mark to qualify for a scholarship. I enclose an application form, should you wish Mia to become a pupil here...*

It was as Ellie had suspected. Although Mia had plenty of ability, she had been in no fit state for such an important exam after the experience she had had with Laurence Finch.

How had she allowed herself to be so taken in by him? Even inviting him to dinner each week? Enjoying his company while all the time he was winning her confidence only to get at Mia.

Maybe she should have taken notice of Noah, who had made no secret of his intense dislike of Laurence Finch.

"Shit! Shit! Shit!" She banged the table in disappointment, but more with rage at herself for being so gullible.

None of this would have happened if Ollie had been alive. Nor would it have happened if Guy Morgan hadn't suggested extra tuition given by his pal, Laurence Finch, whose name he now wanted to protect. Was the reputation of his parish more important than the safety of her daughter?

Should she take the matter further? Would it solve anything? Mia was getting back to her old self, and Ellie didn't want her to be grilled by some stranger, for the trauma to be relived and Mia to revert to where she had been.

She glanced at her watch. Mia and Noah would be home from school any minute. Ellie washed her face, brushed her hair and put on some make-up. She didn't want them to see her anguish and anger.

When Mia and Noah had eaten a snack, Ellie produced the school letter.

"I didn't get the scholarship, did I, Mum?" Mia said. "Don't worry. It's OK. I'll be going to the local school with lots of my friends, and that's fine with me. Don't be disappointed. I'm not. I'm sure Dad also understands."

Mia put her arms around Ellie and hugged her, and then went to her room. Noah scowled and went out to play in the garden with his pal next door.

Chapter 23

The second anniversary of Ollie's sudden death fell on a Sunday, and Ellie, still grieving and after all that had happened with Mia, felt the need for some spiritual consolation. She decided to go to a quiet early morning service and pray for peace and strength for herself.

There was no way she would go to St. Stephen's. The very thought of Guy Morgan made her angry. There was another church in Lislea, St. Olaf's. She googled the parish and saw that they had an eight-thirty said service. Mia and Noah would still be in bed, and she would be back in time for breakfast.

The Revd. Wendy Morris, the rector of St. Olaf's, noticed a new face in the congregation. It wasn't difficult, as the congregation seldom varied.

At the church door after the service, Wendy greeted her usual flock and turned to say hello to Ellie. "You're very welcome to St. Olaf's. My name is Wendy Morris. Are you new to the area?"

"No, I've lived in Lislea for a while, but this is my first time in St. Olaf's. I used to belong to St. Stephen's but...it's a long story. Today is the anniversary of my husband's death and I needed to mark it in some way, religiously, and get a little strength for myself."

"Well, if you ever need someone to talk to, I'm always available. Here, take one of our magazines. You'll find my contact details in it."

Another parishioner was waiting to talk to Wendy, so Ellie just said, "Thanks, thanks very much," and went to get her car.

As she drove home, Ellie was struck by Wendy's quiet manner and the fact that she hadn't probed but had left the door open if Ellie wanted to talk to her.

A contrast to the ever-smiling, over-confident and talkative Guy Morgan.

Chapter 24

For the Revd. John Keble in the nineteenth century, 'the daily round, the common task' furnished all he asked for as a parish priest, or so he said. For the Revd. Jonathan Appleford in the twenty-first century, it furnished more than what he asked for as a curate. There was no let-up in the lists of things he had to do and people he had to visit, amply supplied by his rector, the archdeacon.

Days became weeks, weeks became months. Ministry was relentless. Before he knew it, he had been a year and a half in St. Stephen's.

Although always busy, he was also lonely, and apart from Rosie in the Youth Fellowship and, to a lesser extent, Daniel Norton in the cathedral, he had no real friends.

Friends from theological college days had their own lives and parishes, and in spite of all those promises to keep in touch, it seldom happened. After his English experience, Jonathan had less and less in common with the conservative evangelicals who were once his circle of friends in the Church of Ireland Theological Institute.

He liked Rosie a lot and got on well with her, but he was still unsure about letting their relationship develop into something more serious.

So, when he received an invitation to a party being organised by a friend of Nigel and Patrick, the pair he had spent time with in The Bishop's Apron that night after evensong, he decided to accept. Daniel Norton, the dean's vicar, rang Jonathan to say he was planning to go. "Their parties are something else and not for the faint-hearted. But it's a Friday night, so you should have sobered up by Sunday!"

The Friday night of the party, Jonathan arrived at an apartment in central Dublin, owned by Nigel and Patrick's friend, Dominic.

Jonathan was given a gin and tonic on arrival and was shown into a large room with views over Dublin port. The lights of Sutton and Howth twinkled in the distance. There were about sixteen people in the room, and there seemed to be as many women as men, all around Jonathan's age. Glasses clinked and the conversation buzzed. Pop music played discreetly in the background.

Nigel and Patrick came over to Jonathan and greeted him like an old friend. "You'll probably recognise one or two of the choir," said Nigel. "Those who had the courage to come tonight. And your friend, Laurence Finch, was also invited, but said he couldn't come."

"Not like him when young ladies are around," grinned Patrick. "He has a great eye for pretty young women." He winked, adding, "I heard he goes to one of those 'gentlemen's clubs' in the city centre. At least, that's what I've been told."

Jonathan went over to talk to the choir members he recognised. The majority of those at the party were unknown to him.

Daniel joined him. "Let me give you a warning. Pace yourself with the drinks. Nigel and Patrick are quite liberal with refilling glasses, especially when the drink doesn't belong to them. I've learnt the hard way. Oh, by the way, I have to go in a few moments. I've had a beep from the hospital. I'm sorry to be leaving you, but before I go, I'll introduce you to some of the crowd."

Then, offering his excuses to the host, Daniel left.

Jonathan did his best to make conversation but was finding it difficult. He wasn't in business or finance or consultancy, and he didn't want people to know he was a priest. That would be a sure conversation stopper. He'd had his glass filled up a few times and was beginning to plan his escape when Dominic came into the centre of the room, clapped his hands, turned off the music and announced it was time for party games.

The furniture was pushed back and all were told to sit on the floor in a circle, boy/girl, boy/girl.

"It's time for Truth or Dare," laughed Dominic. "But first, all your glasses have to be refilled with Dominic's Inhibition-Losing Punch."

He produced a box of with folded papers each entitled 'Truth' or 'Dare'. Each person had to close their eyes, choose a paper and then read it to the group.

It all started innocently enough—

"What have you bought that was the biggest waste of money?"

"What is the weirdest dream you ever had?"

—When it came to Jonathan's turn, he drew out a 'Truth'—

"What is something you're glad your mother doesn't know about you?"

—to which he replied, "That I'm here!"

After a few rounds, Dominic gathered in the papers.

"Now for some that are bit more fun. Drain your glasses, it's time for Dominic's Cocktails!" Trays of cocktails were passed around.

Dominic produced another box of folded papers. "Now these are more revealing." There were giggles of anticipation from those in the know.

The box went around. The first guy drew out a 'Dare'—*"Draw a tattoo on the back of the girl on your left."*

Dominic produced a black marker and the girl took off her top and exposed her bare back. There were cheers as the dare was performed.

The girl then drew out a 'Truth'—*"Who would it be if you could kiss someone right now?"* She didn't answer but crawled over to Jonathan and kissed him passionately.

When it came to Jonathan's turn, he drew out a 'Dare'—*"Drink a mystery drink in one go."*

Dominic produced a glass full of clear liquid. The group started clapping and shouting, "Down, down, down!" Jonathan closed his eyes and swallowed the liquid. It burned his throat as it went down.

The girl next to him drew out a 'Dare'—*"Seductively eat a banana whilst locking eyes with the person on your right,"* which happened to be Jonathan, whose face turned bright red as the girl did just that.

His head began to swim. The room began to spin. He was vaguely aware of hoots and hollers and then he slipped into oblivion.

When he regained consciousness—it was four a.m. by his watch—he had a splitting headache. He became aware of a tightness around his head and chest. His legs and feet were cold.

It was then he realised that he was wearing only his boxers and that around his head was stretched a condom and around his chest a lacy bra!

The room was quiet. A few bodies in various states of undress lay asleep on couches or slumped in chairs. He found his clothes in a bundle beside him, dressed quickly and left.

In a daze, he hailed a taxi and went home to St. Stephen's curatage.

Chapter 25

JONATHAN SLUMPED ONTO the sofa in his sitting room and stared into space, utterly humiliated, utterly ashamed and feeling utterly guilty.

Had he gone too far in seeking friendship and company? Why hadn't he taken the hint when Daniel left? Had Daniel *really* received a call from the hospital? Had he known what was planned and made up an excuse to leave? If so, why hadn't he warned Jonathan?

His mind was in a whirl. His head was throbbing. He took some painkillers and went to bed, hoping he could sleep it off and think straighter in the morning. He needed a clear head. He had a sermon to prepare.

But instead of sinking into a deep sleep, he tossed and turned all night, regretting his acceptance of the invitation to Dominic's party and, worse, wondering what on earth he had done while playing 'Truth or Dare'.

He would be the talk of the cathedral choir. He was sure Nigel and Patrick wouldn't spare his blushes and would take pleasure in adding some spice, if that was possible, to how he had behaved at the party.

Dear God, what a mess.

His head was still sore and fuzzy as he got out of bed, showered, dressed and headed to the kitchen to make some breakfast.

His phone pinged.

> Thanks for being such a sport last night. You were the life and soul of the party. Do come again!
> Dominic

If that wasn't bad enough, there followed a photo of Jonathan half-naked, sporting a condom on his head and a lacy bra across his chest.

Worse, Jonathan noticed that the photo had been exchanged on Dominic's WhatsApp posting, and already it had been forwarded to others by members of the group.

Another ping!

> Hi Playboy Priest. Would love to meet up with you sometime. Saucy Sister Selina (the banana girl).
> P.S. Bring my bra with you!!!

He quickly deleted the message and withdrew from the group.

Jonathan went back to see who was on Dominic's WhatsApp group. Yes, just as he feared, Laurence Finch's name was on it. How soon would it be until it was shown to Guy Morgan?

Jonathan poured himself a cup of coffee and sat at the table with his head in his hands.

If word got out, how could he continue in St. Stephen's? He would be the laughing stock not only of the parish and the diocese, but also of the Church. In a small church like the Church of Ireland, everyone knew everyone else, and every bit of scandal was repeated and passed on. What a way to end a short career!

Chapter 26

JONATHAN DRAGGED HIMSELF to church on Sunday morning, feeling like death warmed up. His headache had persisted all Saturday, and when he sat down to write a sermon, there was no inspiration and he turned to a commentary by William Barclay, the last resort of sermon writers, and more or less copied it verbatim.

"You look wretched," remarked Guy Morgan. "Are you sickening for something? Did you do a COVID test?"

"Ah, um," stuttered Jonathan. "No, I never thought of that. I don't know if I have any kit."

"Well, I'll get my wife to give you a box of them after church. Just keep your distance from people. Luckily, you're only preaching this morning, so go home immediately and test yourself and let me know. If you're positive, I don't want you at the staff meeting in the morning."

Guy rang Faith from the vestry and asked her to bring a box of COVID tests for Jonathan.

Jonathan knew from the audible 'tch' from Guy's prayer desk at the end of the sermon that it hadn't gone down too well with his rector. Thankfully, Guy got detained with people after the service, and Jonathan had gone home by the time Guy had returned to the vestry, but he knew he would get an earful in the morning at the staff meeting.

The test was negative and Jonathan texted Guy to say he would be OK to attend Monday's staff meeting. He still had to prepare a talk for the evening youth service, but he was familiar with the formula for such addresses and had plenty of material from talks he'd given while in his home parish.

Jonathan's head was still sore and his stomach was still churning when he arrived at church that evening.

"You look awful," were Rosie's first words as she came into the church. "Are you sickening for something? You shouldn't even be here."

"I'll be all right. I've tested for COVID and it was negative. It'll pass."

"Don't hang around after the service. I'll look after the Youth Fellowship. There are enough leaders to help. Go home and go to bed."

He was about to argue but then realised that if he went home as ordered by Rosie, then there wouldn't be any chat about what he had done over the weekend. Rosie was pretty unshockable, but he would prefer that she didn't know about his antics at the party.

Making his way out of the church after the service, Jonathan saw Guy Morgan and Laurence Finch deep in conversation at the churchyard gate. His heart sank and his stomach started churning again. Things were not looking good.

***

Jonathan had just fixed himself with a stiff gin and tonic when his phone rang. Was it Guy Morgan not wanting to wait until the morning to give him a roasting? He was undecided whether it was a relief when Daniel Norton's name came up on the screen.

Jonathan answered with a wary "Hello?"

"Hope you survived last Friday. By the look of WhatsApp, you had a whale of a time!" Daniel laughed. "Dominic knows how to throw a wild party, eh? And what a fabulous apartment, and the views are to die for. Look, I'm sorry I had to go early and leave you in their clutches. That's the problem about being a hospital chaplain. You never know when you're going to be called. Oops! The dean is trying to get through to me. Heaven knows what he wants at this time of night, but I'd better take his call. Talk soon." And with that, the line went dead.

Jonathan had another sleepless night.

Chapter 27

JONATHAN RANG THE doorbell of the St. Stephen's rectory and was let in by Faith Morgan, who looked at him coldly and, without a word, directed him to her husband's study.

Guy was working on some papers at his desk and without looking up said, "Take a seat." He continued reading for a few minutes and then turned to Jonathan.

"To call yesterday morning's sermon mediocre would be to compliment it. It was straight out of Barclay. I have his commentaries and I checked. It was verbatim. I needn't tell you that I put a great deal of emphasis on the standard of preaching here in St. Stephen's. It's part of our missional strategy. Yesterday's effort did not promote that strategy in any way, but that is the least of my concerns at the moment."

The archdeacon's hard eyes bored into Jonathan. Jonathan looked at the floor.

"It has come to my attention that you attended a party of rather dubious repute last weekend where a lot of alcohol was consumed, and, no doubt, other substances as well. Putting two and two together and getting four, as I usually do, I suspect that your present state is due to excessive drinking and partying. What's more, an image of you in a state of undress with…with… unmentionable items on your person is circulating on social media. Do you realise what a negative image this gives of St. Stephen's and all we stand for? It has made us a laughing stock amongst those who are jealous of our success, and I will not stand for it! I have worked hard to build St. Stephen's into a flagship evangelical church, and I will not have that jeopardised by an immoral, drunken curate.

"I took you on because I thought you were keen and enthusiastic, sympathetic and supportive of all we are doing in St. Stephen's. Apparently, I was misled, for it has also come to my attention that you frequently attend evensong in the cathedral, and, what's more, that you've said it is more to your liking than the worship in St. Stephen's. I feel not only let down but betrayed."

Jonathan continued staring at the floor. He had no excuses.

"Take this as a first, and final, warning. If I don't see an improvement very soon, I will terminate your curacy, and as archdeacon with not a little influence, I will see to it that any vacancy in the diocese of Daneford will be closed to you. Is that understood? Now, pull up your socks, young man, and get back on the straight and narrow. You have been warned."

The rest of the meeting was a blur to Jonathan. He took notes in his diary, which was just as well because by the time he left, he could remember nothing—apart from what Guy had seen and been told—and his warning.

That must've been what Guy Morgan and Laurence Finch had been talking about the previous evening at the church gate. Being on their WhatsApp list, Laurence Finch would have seen the photo, and he'd probably been at evensong in the cathedral and joined the choir in The Bishop's Apron afterwards to hear all the gory details.

But why would he want to shop Jonathan?

Nigel and Patrick were no fans of Laurence Finch. In their efforts to excuse Jonathan's behaviour and to stop Laurence Finch from telling Guy Morgan about the party, had they, perhaps, implied that Jonathan knew about Finch's fancy for pretty girls and about his membership of a men's club in Dublin? Knowing Nigel and Patrick's lack of discretion, maybe they'd told Laurence that Jonathan knew all about him, and Laurence was taking no chances by shopping Jonathan to Guy first.

Jonathan's stomach was churning. It took a lot of effort to get home before throwing up in the toilet.

Guy had left Jonathan with a punishing list of things to do that week. Instead of wallowing in self-pity, he decided to make a start on the long list of pastoral calls that he had been given. If he did them all, it might give him some breathing space before Guy gave him the boot.

There's a lot of give and take in pastoral work. The pastor gives their time and attention but at the end of the visit often goes away with a lot more comfort than they gave.

So, it was when Jonathan visited the ninety-year-old Mrs. Baxter. She lived in a pensioner's bungalow in a quiet cul-de-sac in Lislea.

She had been married for sixty years when her husband died five years previously. Since then, she had experienced a lot of health problems. Her sight deteriorated with macular degeneration, then she was diagnosed with cancer and had to endure major surgery, followed by a course of chemotherapy, which had just been completed.

She was one of life's optimists. A few weeks after being discharged, she threw a party to celebrate her survival, to which her surgeon even dropped in. Jonathan wondered how she could be so cheerful after all she had gone through.

He came away with his spirits slightly lifted. He looked at his list. He might be able to squeeze in two more calls. He would keep busy and maybe it would pass.

But he wasn't so sure it would. His future hung in the balance.

Chapter 28

ONLY TOO PAINFULLY aware that his efforts to find some new friends had failed spectacularly, Jonathan's sense of loneliness deepened. It would be even too embarrassing to go back to the cathedral for evensong. They would all have heard of his escapades at Dominic's party. He squirmed with embarrassment every time he met Guy Morgan. While he worked hard, his heart wasn't in it. His only solace was a drink each night at the end of the day—to help him sleep.

At the end of the service the following Sunday, Laurence Finch came over to him, all smiles. "Wonderful sermon this morning, Jonathan. Plenty to think about in what you said. I could see that Guy approved."

What a hypocrite! Jonathan thought to himself and smiled wanly. Now he knew for sure it was Laurence Finch who'd told Guy about the party.

Over the weeks that followed, no matter how hard he tried, Jonathan couldn't muster up the motivation to do anything in St. Stephen's and squirmed whenever he was in the presence of Guy Morgan.

Laurence Finch acted all pally after morning services—"I've had COVID myself. Took me weeks to feel right again"—but Jonathan couldn't shake the thought that Laurence had only shopped him to protect his own reputation and standing with his rector. As a great rugby player had once excused himself for rough play, he was 'getting his retaliation in first'.

When Rosie saw Jonathan later at the youth service, her shock was palpable. They knew each other well enough by now for her to have picked up that there was something was troubling him. "Have you time for a cup of coffee and a chat after the Youth Fellowship?" she asked.

"Yes, that would be good. I'd like that," replied Jonathan. Rosie was the only person he could trust, the only person in whom he could confide, and a coffee and chat might be better than a drink on his own.

She sat quietly at the kitchen table while he made coffee and brought it over.

He sat opposite her, looking down at the table, his hands clasped around his mug. After what seemed like an eternity, he looked up. "I've made the most horrible mistake of my life."

"You can tell me what it is," she encouraged gently. "With my family background, I'm pretty unshockable."

Jonathan paused to gather his wits, and then the whole story came out—his visits to the cathedral, meeting up with choir in The Bishop's Apron, the invitation to Dominic's party.

"I've deleted the photo—it was not very flattering—but Guy Morgan has heard all about it and seen the evidence. As you might guess, he's not too impressed. I've been given a rollicking and told that my next misstep will be my last. He'll fire me!"

"But *how* did Guy Morgan hear about the party?" asked Rosie. "He's not very involved with the cathedral, and he and the dean don't get on at all. Who would have squealed on you?"

"There can only be one person. Laurence Finch! He knocks about with the choir in The Bishop's Apron after evensong—he used to be in the cathedral choir. He's on their WhatsApp group, and apparently, he was invited to the party but didn't turn up. I think two of the choir members who don't like him may have intimated they told me some not very nice things about him, and this is his way of keeping me quiet."

"I never did like that man. He gives me the creeps. He looks at me as if he's undressing me." Rosie shuddered for effect. "What are you going to do?"

"What can I do? Keep my bib clean. I'm over two years in St. Stephen's, so it will soon be time to be thinking of a move, but Guy Morgan has already told me that he will block any move in Daneford and the surrounding dioceses."

Rosie reached out and took his hand. "Poor you. Everyone makes mistakes, but it appears forgiveness is not very high on Guy Morgan's list of Christian virtues."

They sat looking at each other. Rosie got up and stood behind his chair with her arms around his shoulders and held her head close to his. He wanted to get up and embrace her, but he hesitated too long and the moment passed.

"I'd better be on my way," said Rosie, straightening up. "Don't forget that I'm here if you need me."

He heard the front door close.

"Damn, damn, damn!" he muttered to himself. "Why am I pushing away the one person who understands me? It's a pity I wasn't as cautious at that party!"

Chapter 29

A FEW WEEKS LATER, Jonathan got back in one evening after a pastoral call and was about to pour himself a glass of wine when the phone rang.

Reluctantly, he answered it.

"Hello, is that Jonathan Appleford? This is Andrew Caldwell. You may remember my visits to the Theological Institute for the occasional lecture?"

"Yes, yes, I do," replied Jonathan cautiously. He remembered Andrew and his lectures on the philosophy of religion. Well, he remembered Andrew more than he did what he taught.

"You probably know that I'm now the bishop of a conglomerate of dioceses in the deep south of the country? A new experience for me after years in Dublin suburbia." He laughed. "However, the purpose of my call is not to update you on my ecclesiastical career. I was talking to your rector at a meeting in Church House last week."

Jonathan's stomach clenched. He waited.

"Guy Morgan said he thought you were ready for a move and said a more rural parish might be good for you. Give you a broader experience of the Church of Ireland. He spoke highly of your ability and gave you a warm recommendation."

The dark arts of being an archdeacon!

"Well, as it happens, I have a vacancy in the diocese that might suit you," Andrew continued. "It's got four churches but only two regular morning services—in the two bigger churches. The other two have a monthly evening service.

The numbers attending would be nothing like St. Stephen's, even with Guy's *evangelastic* counting." The bishop laughed again. "But the parishioners are faithful and committed, and they would welcome a young man like you. What do you say?"

"Well, um, I'm grateful to you, Bishop, for thinking of me. It's come as a bit of a surprise. Can I take a few days to think about it? Where exactly is the parish you're talking about?"

"Oh, forgive me," said the bishop. "I should have told you that at the beginning. The two main churches are in the villages of Inchymore and Inchybeg, and the rectory is in one of the other villages, Kilcadam. I could meet you down there, treat you to lunch and give you a tour. It's a beautiful part of the country. May I give you a ring back in a few days' time when you have had some time to think about it? And, of course, pray about it."

"I'm off on Saturday, and I will be around all day," said Jonathan.

"Good man. I'll ring you around lunchtime on Saturday," The bishop rang off.

Was this the glimmer of light that Jonathan had hoped and prayed would pierce the darkness that had enveloped him? Even though he knew Guy was only trying to get rid of him, maybe this would be a way out of the mess he had got himself into, to cut ties with Daneford and Dublin and put the events of the past behind him.

Chapter 30

Ellie Jones had returned to St. Olaf's for the early morning communion service and readily agreed to Wendy Morris's offer to meet for a cup of coffee. Ellie had a day off coming up and suggested that Wendy come to her house.

Noticing all the photos of Ollie in the lounge, Wendy asked about him.

"Ollie died three years ago," replied Ellie. "It was one of those sudden death syndromes. Ollie was very fit and still playing rugby."

Wendy was a good listener and gave Ellie space to talk about Ollie, Mia and Noah, and of her hopes to be able to send Mia to her old fee-paying school.

And then Ellie told Wendy of Guy Morgan's suggestion of extra tuition given by Laurence Finch.

"He's the principal of your school, isn't he?" asked Ellie. "What do you make of him?"

Wendy laughed ruefully. "I'm afraid we don't see eye to eye on many things, so I'm not the best person to ask. I know Guy Morgan has a high regard for him."

"That's no great recommendation then," Ellie shot back bitterly. She then told Wendy what had happened with Mia.

"You should tell Guy Morgan," said Wendy, shocked at what she was being told.

"Oh, I did. And all he could say was that Mia must have imagined it. Laurence Finch was such a good man, he said. He was sure Mia was fantasising."

"But that should be reported to the diocesan safeguarding officer."

"Guy Morgan said no one would believe us and that we would be dragging St. Stephen's, and the Church, into disrepute. We would be ruining a distinguished career. He told me to drop it."

"But you shouldn't," Wendy insisted. "It goes against all that we have been advised to do in such situations. And Guy Morgan should be worried more about Mia than Laurence Finch."

"I'm reluctant to take it any further," admitted Ellie. "Mia seems to have got over it, though she was a handful for some time. I don't want to drag it all up again for her sake. Funny, I thought at first that Laurence Finch was a really nice person, and so did Mia. He stayed behind for a few meals with us after lessons. He even took the kids to the cinema and McDonald's afterwards. Noah never liked him. Perhaps my son is a better judge of people than Mia or me."

"Well, if you reconsider and need some support, you can rely on me," Wendy assured her. "But I do need to tell the diocesan safeguarding officer even if you don't want to do anything. I'll put in a written report and we'll see what they say."

"Is that really necessary?" Ellie looked worried.

"Yes, I'm afraid it is. There's no opt-out. But I will explain your wishes when I write." Wendy glanced at her watch. "I'm afraid I have to go. I have someone coming to see me in a short while, and as I live on my own, I'd better be there to let them in."

"I really don't want to take any legal steps about this. Can you make that clear? If it has to be recorded, so be it, but I don't want anything done about it."

"I'll talk to the safeguarding officer and explain the situation." Wendy got up to leave.

"Thanks so much for calling and for listening to me rabbiting on. I never asked you about yourself. Maybe some other time?"

"Yes, I would enjoy that," said Wendy. "And you, and the children, are very welcome anytime in St. Olaf's."

***

As she drove away, Wendy reflected on what Ellie had told her. The detective inspector who had investigated the murder of her organist had told her about Laurence Finch's connection with the dubious men's club in Dublin. But this was much worse.

"The bastard!" she hissed. She was brought back to the present by horns blaring as she realised that she had driven through traffic lights that had just turned red.

Chapter 31

"INCHYMORE AND INCHYBEG are two prosperous villages," said Bishop Andrew as he and Jonathan sat down for lunch in the Inchymore Hotel. "Actually, Inchymore is a small town rather than a village, as you can see. Many of your parishioners here are farmers, and this gives great stability to the parish. Others run small businesses. The supermarket is owned by a parishioner, and another runs a weaving factory, another has a pottery and so on. Then some run B and Bs. In the summer, Inchymore has a lot of tourists passing through."

Jonathan had thought, and he had tried to pray, about Bishop Andrew's offer. He knew he had no future in St. Stephen's, nor in the diocese of Daneford as long as Guy Morgan was archdeacon.

The area around Inchymore and Inchybeg was beautiful. Bishop Andrew had not exaggerated. The two villages were situated on either side of an inlet, washed by the Atlantic Ocean. It was remote, but Jonathan felt that here, he could leave his past behind and start afresh, away from the cathedral crowd and far away from Guy Morgan.

When the bishop had rung on Friday lunchtime, Jonathan had made up his mind and accepted the offer to meet, so here they were, taking a tour of the parishes and surrounding area.

Bishop Andrew was bright and breezy and full of enthusiasm as a new bishop. He talked up the parish as well as any estate agent trying to sell a dilapidated house with 'potential to develop'. They visited the churches, which the bishop had arranged to be left open. They were all rather plain, Semple-like churches of the nineteenth century, though one, Kilcadam, beside the imposing Kilcadam Hall, was very pretty. While not an estate church, it was maintained by the Hamilton's of Kilcadam Hall. The tablets on the walls were all in memory of various scions of the Hamilton family, and on the altar, a beautiful silver cross and two candlesticks had also been given by the Hamiltons.

"The Hamiltons are not as wealthy or influential as they once were," said the bishop. "They sold off most of their land to maintain the hall and their lifestyle. In fact, the only member of the family left now is Marjorie—an elderly spinster and the last of the line. You'll get to know her well enough. She never misses a service in Kilcadam Church. I believe the last rector tried to close the church, but such was Marjorie's opposition—and threats—that he gave up in the end. Not surprisingly, it is strictly BCP.

"The rectory is also here in Kilcadam, so we'll go there next."

***

"Now I don't want you to be put off by first appearances," said the bishop as they approached the gateway to a long, overgrown avenue that led up to the rectory. "It's actually a lovely house. Look at it as what it will become rather than what it is at present. It's been vacant for a few years, but the vestry has put aside a considerable amount of money to do it up, and parishioners will come in with machinery and clear up the garden and grounds. They are only waiting for a new incumbent to be appointed, and then they will start the work."

The bishop had not exaggerated about the state of the grounds. High beech hedges lined the avenue, which was little more than a grass-covered track that terminated outside a solid but briar-strangled Georgian house. Bishop Andrew took out some keys and, with some difficulty, opened the front door.

"The last rector was Canon Watson, who lived here with his wife and sister-in-law. He went on until he was seventy-five, so you can imagine that in his later years, he did little to maintain the rectory and grounds. The vestry offered their help many times, but he was fiercely independent and probably embarrassed over the state of the house, and he always refused their help. But, as I say, there's nothing that cannot be updated and rectified."

The house felt musty and stale. One wing, probably the servants' quarters in the 'good old days', was blocked off. One thing the canon had let them do was to install central heating, which was about the only good thing about the house. The two reception rooms on either side of the hall were large, and before the hall led into the kitchen, there was a smaller room which could be used as a study-cum-den. Upstairs, the bedrooms were equally large, while the bathroom was situated on the turn of the stairs.

The brambles had reached the back door, and Jonathan could just make out what was once a pebbled yard leading through a gate to the lawn, which was like a meadow.

"It's got potential," said the bishop, sounding like Capability Brown. "The fields around the rectory are owned by the parish and they are let out. The income is ear-marked for the upkeep of the rectory, so renovation won't be a problem. I know it looks a bit of a mess at the moment, but it will be a beautiful house once the work is done. And I will make sure they spend what is needed. I promise you that."

They made their way back to the bishop's car. "I've got to get back to the See House for a meeting, so I will drop you off at the Inchymore Hotel. That is where your car is? And I'll see that you are refunded the cost of petrol and so on. I know you have a lot to take in and consider, but I would love to have you in the diocese, and I'll ring you in a few days' time to discuss it further."

***

Driving back to Lislea, Jonathan pondered what he should do and concluded that he didn't really have many options. In fact, he reasoned, they came down to two.

One: give up ministry altogether. But what else was he trained to do? He would also have to explain the reason to his parents, and that might open a can of worms that he was determined should remain shut.

Two: take the bishop's offer of Inchymore. He didn't seem to want to probe into Jonathan's past, and with the appointment being the bishop's, there was no nomination board to face.

It wasn't the kind of parish he had hoped for, but that was before that dreadful party. The fact that the parish was vacant for over two years meant no one else was interested in it. It was his for the taking, and he really did need a fresh start away from all that had happened. And if Bishop Andrew's promises were kept, he would have a rather grand house to live in.

When the bishop rang, Jonathan accepted the parish. Bishop Andrew said he was delighted and would talk to Guy Morgan about a release date, and that he would get the vestry moving on repairs and renovations.

Guy Morgan informed Bishop Andrew that Jonathan could go whenever the bishop wanted. He didn't want to stand in the way of his curate's preferment.

Chapter 32

Jonathan's institution service was arranged for two months later. Guy continued to heap the work on Jonathan, and Jonathan's days off were spent looking for furniture to fill the spacious Kilcadam rectory.

Rosie offered to help, and they trudged around auction rooms and second-hand furniture stores. It was a distraction for Jonathan—and Rosie—and he enjoyed her company and her help. It seemed she had come to accept that, from Jonathan's point of view, the relationship was platonic rather than romantic.

Very few clergy from Daneford diocese attended his institution. Guy Morgan sent his apologies, saying he had to attend a diocesan planning meeting that had been in his diary for months. Wendy Morris went, as she had heard from Ellie Jones that a rumour was going around that there had been a breakdown in relations between Guy and Jonathan. The speed of the move confirmed this and also gave Wendy an excuse to visit her mother, who lived about halfway between Lislea and Inchymore.

There had been no contact from Daniel Norton, the dean's vicar in Daneford Cathedral. No doubt he had heard the full story of the party and was lying low, not wishing to be tainted by supporting Jonathan.

The five other clergy in Jonathan's new diocese all attended the service, as did a few from the other seven dioceses in Bishop Andrew's episcopal care.

Jonathan's parents and a few of their friends came from Northern Ireland. The plan was for them to stay in the newly refurbished rectory, but though the work had been started, it wasn't finished, and the place was covered in dust. They opted to stay in the Inchymore Hotel.

His parents tried to show they were happy with Jonathan's 'promotion', but he could tell they were wondering why he had taken a parish in the back of beyond and had not chosen to look for 'a wee parish' in the North.

Rosie had also come down from Dublin for the institution, and while she would have been quite content to camp in an unfinished room in the rectory, she reckoned it would cause a bit of gossip, which was what Jonathan definitely didn't need.

Inchymore Church was full. Jonathan's new parishioners turned out in force to see who they were getting as their new rector, as did a few nosey people from neighbouring parishes.

A choir of sorts had been cobbled together for the service, and while they led the singing in a hearty manner, their motets during communion were wobbly and warbly—a far cry from the music that had so entranced him in Cambridge and Liverpool.

There would be no liturgical flights of fancy in the Inchymore Union of Parishes.

Chapter 33

Sometimes in St. Stephen's Jonathan might have had to do three services on a Sunday, but apart from the eight a.m. communion, there had always been someone else taking part, and he hadn't had to preach every week.

In Inchymore, he had two morning services, at ten and eleven-thirty a.m., and twice a month an evening service at one of the other two churches.

He had to lead the worship and preach the same sermon at all the services. Sometimes the sermon seemed to go well in one church but felt stilted in another, and by the third time he came to preach the same sermon, even he was bored with it.

In Inchymore, there was a small organ and an organist who played the right notes and sometimes in the right order. In all the other churches, there was recorded music, played by a member of the congregation with varying degrees of competency.

There was little time for chat between the two morning services, as he had to drive five miles from one to the other. Nor was there time to dawdle and admire the scenery. 'The quick and the dead' took on a new meaning as Jonathan sped between services.

He'd arranged to meet with the churchwardens on the Monday evening following his first Sunday in Inchymore. They came to his half-finished, half-furnished rectory with goody bags from their wives for their new bachelor rector. Jonathan was supplied with prepared meals, homemade bread and cake.

Sitting uncomfortably on plastic chairs in the sitting room, they apologised for the slowness of the renovations and promised to put pressure on the builder to get it all finished as soon as possible.

There was no list of parishioners, so Jonathan asked them to compile a list of names and addresses, phone numbers and email addresses for the members of each church.

A full meeting of the vestry was organised. Thankfully, in the vacancy, Bishop Andrew had got them to agree to become a union of parishes with one vestry rather than a group with four vestries.

Jonathan asked for a list of those who were sick or in hospital or who might need a pastoral call.

"You might want to give Dara and Tom Wardle a call. They've just been released from jail, and it would be good to reassure them that the Church has forgiven them and that they are welcome at services," said Charlie Daly from Kilcadam.

"What were they in for?" asked Jonathan.

"Oh, nothing serious," replied Charlie. "It's just that they put some cyanide in the river to stun the salmon and make it easier to catch them. There's a lot of money in fresh salmon. It's unfortunate that they were caught by the bailiff."

"But they are really good lads," said the other churchwarden. "If you need anything practical done—trees felled, sheds repaired, engines fixed—Dara and Tom are the ones to ask."

"And they're good shots with a rifle," Charlie continued. "We had a problem with a pigeon who got into Inchybeg Church. We tried everything to get it out. The pews were covered with its droppings, even the communion table. In the end, we asked Dara and Tom, and they got rid of the pigeon."

"How?" asked Jonathan.

"They shot it."

Ministry in Inchymore was going to be different, a far cry from anything he had experienced so far.

Chapter 34

It was time to visit Marjorie Hamilton of Kilcadam Hall. It shouldn't be left too long as, after all, he was a kind of neighbour with the rectory also in Kilcadam.

Imposing gates led off the small village square, up a long avenue of overgrown laurels and rhododendrons, to a big block of a Georgian house at least double, if not treble, the size of the rectory, and Jonathan had thought that was huge.

He walked up the granite steps to the front door and pulled the bell, half expecting to be greeted by a maid or a butler. However, the door was opened by Marjorie Hamilton herself, a grey-haired, rather plump, seventy-five-year-old dressed in an old-fashioned woollen twin suit. Expensive pearls hung around her neck. Behind the gold-rimmed glasses, Jonathan could see lively, determined eyes.

"Ah, Rector, I was wondering when you would call. Do come in."

Beyond the front door was a dimly lit hall with heavy, dark furniture. Over the oak-stained floorboards was a series of fresh planks leading into various rooms off the hall.

"Mind your step. Keep to the plank on your left. We have a major problem with rising damp, which has rotted the floor joists. But so far, the drawing room is safe.

"I'm afraid the wealth of the Hamiltons is not what it was. We sold land to try to maintain the hall, but it's a losing battle. Now I just have to make do. Anyway, when I'm gone, the whole place will be sold and probably be knocked down for an estate of new, vulgar houses for the locals."

They entered the drawing room, which was bright and airy with a view of the sea. Sofas and armchairs were strewn around the room. In the corner stood a full-sized harp. Photos of Hamiltons competed for space on side tables, and portraits of the clan hung on the walls, along with the occasional landscape.

"Will you have tea?" asked Marjorie. "I have Chinese, Indian, Kenyan and Moroccan. Which do you prefer?"

"Oh, ah, um…" Jonathan was flummoxed. He hadn't a clue, but knew he had to make a quick choice. The phrase 'all the tea in China' came into his head. "Chinese, please."

He sat in the armchair she had indicated and waited, looking around a room that was straight out of *National Trust Magazine*.

Marjorie arrived back with a silver tray of delicate China cups and plates and some digestive biscuits.

She poured the tea and sat down opposite him. "Now, Rector," she said, "I'll get straight down to business so that there may be no misunderstanding between us. Whereas Kilcadam Church is not strictly an estate church, it has been generously supported and maintained by the Hamilton family for many generations. As you have probably noticed, there are many Hamilton memorials on the walls of the church, and the cross and candlesticks on the altar were given in memory of my father, Brigadier-General Arthur Hamilton. So I have a deep affection for Kilcadam and will be buried there, along with my forebears, when my time comes."

Jonathan said nothing.

"I might add," Marjorie continued, "that I have resisted all attempts to close Kilcadam Church in the past and will continue to do so in the future should the need arise." She fixed him with a stony stare. "The previous bishop knew my views, and we had reached an agreement for my lifetime. I am sure the new bishop will honour that agreement. They can implement their so-called parish renewal plans elsewhere, but not here—as long as I have breath in me."

Jonathan sat there in silence. It was like being lectured as a new boy in school by an overbearing teacher.

"Now, what are your liturgical tastes?"

"Well, in my upbringing, I was a low-church evangelical. But when I went to Cambridge, I got to like the more high church liturgy and practice. I suppose, now, I would describe myself as a Liberal Catholic."

"I'm glad to hear. I had my doubts when I read that you had been a curate at St. Stephen's, Daneford. The news about suburban churches seeps down even here, and I have not been a fan of your rector and archdeacon, Guy Morgan, and his modernising ways.

"We are firmly *Book of Common Prayer* here in Kilcadam and will continue to be so. The banality of the language in modern services offends me. We are a small congregation, but I do like things to be done decently and in order."

With his card well and truly marked, and with no discussion invited, Marjorie sat back. "You say that you spent some time in Cambridge. How did you find that experience? I, myself, am a graduate of Girton."

Jonathan relaxed slightly. At least the latter part of his visit to Kilcadam Hall might be a dialogue rather than a monologue.

Chapter 35

THE FIRST FEW months passed quickly for Jonathan. The workmen finished the renovations. Spring rolled into summer, the evenings were bright, and the sun, when it wasn't hidden by rain clouds, was warm.

The farmers among his parishioners, true to Bishop Andrew's word, came with their tractors and machinery and cleared the rectory grounds and cut back the hedges, revealing what had once been a well-kept garden.

Dara and Tom sourced a second-hand ride-on mower for Jonathan, who spent many happy and contented hours cutting the grass and preventing it becoming a wilderness again.

The scenery was impressive as he drove around the parish, finding where his parishioners lived. Behind the fine sandy beaches of the inlet, fertile fields ran up to hills and mountains, which always seemed to look different depending on the season and the weather. Sometimes they could be dark and threatening, at other times bright and welcoming.

The locals had a saying: *"If you can't see the mountains, it's raining. If you can see the mountains, it's just about to rain."* But there were sunny, balmy, Mediterranean-type days as well.

The towns and villages were busy with tourists during the summer, and there were all kinds of festivals held. The pubs and restaurants did a roaring trade during these. The summer kept them solvent for the rest of the year when all was quiet.

Inchymore had a festival of Irish music and culture, and Jonathan, as the new rector, was invited to take part.

Charlie Daly, the churchwarden, suggested to Jonathan that it would be really good if he could say a few words in Irish to begin his speech.

"But I'm from Northern Ireland," protested Jonathan. "Protestants don't learn Irish in school there. I don't have a clue about Irish or how it's pronounced."

"But it would be a feather in your cap if you could," persisted Charlie. "I'll tell you what. My sister is a teacher and she'll give you a few sentences in Irish and write them out phonetically. I'll get her to come round and give you a lesson." There was no arguing!

The following Sunday, Charlie handed Jonathan a piece of paper and told him that his sister would be with them on Wednesday evening. "Come for dinner at six-thirty, and she'll put you through your paces. Have a go at what she has written down. She'll make sure you pronounce it properly."

That evening, Jonathan unfolded the piece of paper and looked at it with incomprehension.

He had come across 'speaking in tongues' while at college, and had, he believed, even spoken in tongues himself. But glossolalia was effortless compared to what was in front of him. He was more nervous about trying to speak Irish than he was about giving his first sermon.

He looked again.

> *Is more an onore a vet eh lawher air on ocawd spesheelta shuh, og us bah wah lum bwee o cas a gowall dun cushda a hug an cwera shuh dum. Is eh mo gwee go rev clew og us cawl air on ocawd shuh og us go rev shay eh gwivneh na deeney guh fada an law.*

In the weeks before the festival, those words became a mantra. He repeated them before sleeping and first thing on waking up. He went over and over them while driving his car around the parish.

It went down extremely well at the festival. "That's a fine Donegal blas you have," said the chairman. "Well done." And he might have added, "For a Protestant."

Could there be higher praise?

According to Charlie's sister, what Jonathan had said in his 'fine Donegal blas'—or dialect—was:

> *It's a great honour to be present at this special occasion, and I would like to say thank you to the committee who invited me. I hope that the festival will go well and that it will be remembered for a long time.*

At least, Jonathan would remember it for the rest of his life.

Chapter 36

THE NEWS SPREAD around Lislea like wildfire. Laurence Finch had been murdered!

His body had been found down a side street in Dublin near the Sunset Strip Gentlemen's Club.

It looked as if he had been mugged, but his wallet had not been stolen nor his expensive watch, but he had certainly been roughed up and had received a fatal blow to the head.

The police were treating his death as 'suspicious'. Detective Chief Inspector Frank Mulready was heading up the investigation.

From a previous case—the murder of Wendy Morris's organist, Ian Wilson—the police had already discovered that the Sunset Strip was owned and run by paramilitaries from Northern Ireland to launder money from their drug activities.

They had also discovered that Laurence Finch was a member and on the committee running the club—a position he had not disclosed to his friend and rector, Guy Morgan.

DCI Mulready rang the bell of St. Olaf's rectory.

"Well, look who it is! I have been half expecting that you might call," the Revd. Wendy Morris said as she opened the door to the DCI. "Do come in. Coffee?"

DCI Mulready sat in Wendy's kitchen as she brewed the coffee.

"I imagine this is not a social call?" laughed Wendy. "Having solved the murder of poor Ian Wilson, are you now on the case of Laurence Finch? Am I a suspect?"

"No, not at the moment, although that could change," joked the inspector. "But you were very helpful in the case of Ian Wilson. So, I thought I'd call round and refresh my memory of your dealings with Laurence Finch."

"Well, as you know, Laurence Finch wasn't all that he appeared to be," replied Wendy. "And, as you also know, I certainly had my differences with him in his role as principal of St. Olaf's School, as did some of the more independent-minded parents. He had a violent temper, and despite being a paid-up member of St. Stephen's, there was a dark side to his character."

"Indeed." Mulready had a serious look on his face. "He was also a member of the Sunset Strip and on their organising committee, as I think I told you last time, and whereas we think his death may have been associated with his involvement there—the paramilitaries who own it would think nothing of disposing of those who get in their way—I want to build up as full a picture as possible of Laurence Finch. Is there anything else I should know school-wise or church-wise?"

"Actually, things have quietened for me in school. My relationship with Laurence had become more workable than before. It was still frosty rather than friendly, but we'd had no great fallings out. We were in a squall-free period for a change."

"And church-wise?" asked the DCI.

Wendy hesitated. Should she mention what Ellie had told her about Laurence Finch and Mia? She decided not to. It had been told in confidence. However well Wendy got on with Frank Mulready, she knew he would follow that up, and it would shatter the pastoral relationship that was building up between Wendy and Ellie and could set Mia back.

"The curate of St. Stephen's, Jonathan Appleford, left suddenly a few months ago. Seemingly, it wasn't his choice to go. The story is that his rector, Guy Morgan, put pressure on him to leave after Laurence Finch told Guy about some wild party that Jonathan had been seen at. Apparently, Jonathan was hungover for a few days afterwards, and Guy tore strips off him. The relationship broke down, and Jonathan was told in no uncertain terms to get out, and the further away from St. Stephen's and Daneford the better. He ended up in Inchymore, in the back of beyond."

"Shopped by Laurence Finch!" mused Frank Mulready. "He wasn't one to take the high moral ground."

"That's the story that's going around. It has a ring of truth, though, because Guy loses no opportunity to blacken Jonathan's reputation. In that respect, Guy is not unlike Laurence Finch."

"You've been very helpful, as usual." Frank rose to go. "We're concentrating on the Sunset Strip connection at the moment, but you never know. I'll keep in touch."

Wendy saw him to the door and returned to her study. "What is it with me and murders?" she wondered.

Chapter 37

DCI Frank Mulready went to call on the Ven. Guy Morgan, rector of St. Stephen's. Guy brought the DCI into his study.

"No doubt you have come to ask me about Laurence Finch," smiled Guy. "What an awful thing to happen to such a good man. He was the backbone of the parish. Such a support to me in all we tried to do from the day we arrived five years ago. Always there to back me up."

"But he wasn't popular with everyone," DCI Mulready commented.

"No indeed!" retorted Guy, with anger in his voice. "There's that Wendy Morris for a start, challenging him about everything in St. Olaf's School, turning parents against him and trying to make out he was a thief just because a school account was in his sole name. It was a bit irregular, but it was only for emergencies and for use in between board meetings. It was all accounted for, but she made a big thing out of it. I know I shouldn't say it, but I find it difficult to forgive her for all the trouble she caused him."

"So you had no reason to doubt Mr Finch's integrity?" asked the DCI.

"No, none at all," said the archdeacon. "He was always open and honest. He had the good of St. Stephen's at heart. In fact, it was he who alerted me to the misbehaviour of my former curate, the Reverend Jonathan Appleford."

"And what was that?"

"According to what Laurence heard and told me, Jonathan got himself invited to a party that some of the younger choir members were going to. It was one of those drink-and-drug-fuelled nights and was followed by a photo of my curate on social media." He took out his phone and scrolled through his photos. "Here, take a look at that! The curate of St. Stephen's! Laurence was shocked when he saw it and thought it his duty to tell me. So loyal. We'll put together a fitting service for him."

"How did Mr. Finch get a copy of that photo?" asked Mulready.

"Laurence kept up with the choir in the cathedral. He was a choirboy there in his early days, and some of his contemporaries still sing in the choir. He didn't much care for that kind of service anymore but liked to support his friends and meet up with them from time to time.

"Jonathan Appleford went to evensong there regularly and went drinking with some of the choir afterwards. Not that he told me. He turned out to be a sly one. Anyway, it seems that one of the choir members passed on the photo to Laurence, knowing that he was a member of St. Stephen's."

"And Mr. Finch passed it on to you?"

"Correct."

"Did Mr. Appleford know how you got hold of the photo?" asked the DCI.

"No! I made sure that my source was not named. Anyway, Appleford was so shocked and humiliated that he asked no questions. I admit I gave him a severe talking-to." Guy sat back, pleased with himself. "He has since moved to an isolated parish in the southwest. It's what he deserves. I made sure he was not going to stay in Daneford."

The DCI looked around the walls of the archdeacon's study. They were full of photos of Guy with what Mulready presumed were important ecclesiastics. One wall, behind Guy's desk, had photos of Guy as a young man in cricket gear and beneath them a cricket bat and a colours cap.

"I see that you were a cricketer in your young day," remarked Mulready.

"Ah, yes," replied Guy smugly. "I played for my school's first eleven. We won the cup that year—that's my captain's cap."

"That bat looks well-used. You must have hit a few sixes with that."

"Yes, it's been around and has got a bit battered. Do you play yourself?" asked the archdeacon.

Mulready laughed. "No, cricket was a foreigner's game where I come from. We all played Gaelic football and hurling. Though I hear cricket is making a comeback in some of the rural areas. It's too slow of a game for me." The DCI got up. "I mustn't keep you any longer. You've been most helpful."

Chapter 38

When Mia and Noah came home from school, their mother, Ellie, sat them down at the kitchen table for their after-school snack.

"I've some news for you both, especially for you, Mia." She paused. The children gave her their full attention. "Mr Finch was attacked and killed in Dublin last night."

"Yes!!" Noah punched the air with his fist. "He was a horrible man and horrible to Mia. I'm not a bit sorry," and turning to Mia, "and you shouldn't be sorry either." He touched her arm in a rare show of brotherly love.

"No, I'm not sorry," Mia said defiantly. "He…he…"

"We don't need to go into all that now," Ellie said quickly. "But I thought you should know. You'll hear it anyway. And… I'm not sorry either."

Later that night, Ellie's phone rang. "Hello, Ellie, this is Wendy Morris from St. Olaf's. I presume you have heard the news about Laurence Finch?"

"Yes, it's all over the town. Led by Guy Morgan, Laurence Finch is being exalted to being a saint already. Little do they know! But don't worry, I'm not going to say anything. I've told Mia and Noah. Well, they're going to hear it at school."

"How did they take it?" asked Wendy.

"Noah is delighted. He never did like Laurence Finch. Thought he was creepy. But then, he doesn't like any teacher."

"And Mia?"

"She didn't say much. She's a deep one. But I think she's all right. We had a bit of a chat when she went to bed this evening. She's getting over the whole trauma of it, and I don't want to really rake it all up again."

"Look, I know it's late, but I just wanted to know how you all are. I'll keep in touch. Good night, Ellie."

***

No sooner had Wendy finished the call than her phone rang. Guy Morgan's name flashed up on the screen. With a sigh, she answered the call.

"Wendy, this is Guy Morgan here. I presume you've heard of the tragic death of Laurence Finch? I know you had your differences with him as principal of your school, and you're probably not too sorry he's gone—"

"Hold on, Guy," Wendy interrupted. "That's rather a sweeping statement—or rather, *accusation*—to make."

"Whatever," Guy resumed. "Laurence Finch was a good friend to St. Stephen's and to me. I hope you can bring yourself to come to his funeral as chair of the board of management. You needn't robe if you don't want to, but I expect that you will close St. Olaf's school for the day as a mark of respect. I will reserve some pews near the front for your sixth-class pupils. I hope that's understood?"

"Parents have already been notified that St. Olaf's is closed for the day of the funeral," replied Wendy coolly. "Sixth class have already been asked to attend, and I will be there with them and see them into their allotted pews. And I will robe."

The line went dead.

"You bastard!" Wendy said out loud as the 'call finished' sign disappeared.

Chapter 39

Jonathan was chairing a meeting of the select vestry of Inchymore when his phone pinged. Much as he was tempted to have a quick peek at the screen, he knew he couldn't in full view of the members who sat in front of him, and the honorary secretary and treasurer were at either elbow.

They were in the middle of having a lively discussion about bats in one of the smallest and most far-flung churches of the group, Kiltraugh.

As the name suggested, the church was situated across the road from the beach that ran along the inlet around which Jonathan's parish was situated. It was a bleak place in winter, but in the summer, it was packed with day-trippers and the occupants of the nearby large caravan park. Occasionally one or two holidaymakers popped in for the monthly evening service. Otherwise, the only evidence for the influx of visitors was the bags of rubbish, empty beer cans and needles in the grounds of the church.

And now, to add to the woes of the very few parishioners of Kiltraugh, there was the presence of bats. It was not so much the bats themselves but the mess they made inside the church.

"It's tight enough to get to open the church after milking," said Bertie Canavan, a Kiltraugh stalwart, "without me and Hilda having to clean the church before the service as well. We have to do something to get rid of them."

"I suppose they are too small and too quick for Tom and Dara to have a shot at?" asked churchwarden, Charlie Daly, only half-joking.

"Actually," the honorary secretary, Maureen Lonergan, said with authority, "I have heard of two ways to rid churches of bats. I knew it was coming up on the agenda, and I've been doing a bit of research."

She smiled condescendingly and there was silence.

Maureen laid down her pen and straightened her shoulders. "Gorse and owls!" she proclaimed.

"But we're talking about the inside of the church," spluttered Bertie. "We can't start growing gorse bushes inside the church, and sure, the owls would make as much of a mess as the bats!"

"I've thought of that." She smiled again. "You see, from what I've researched, gorse bushes interfere with the flight path of bats, so what I'm suggesting is that we hang some cut gorse from the rafters to confuse them. After that, they'll probably leave."

Maureen sat back triumphantly.

"And where do owls come in?" asked Bertie, unconvinced.

Maureen sat up again. "Bats are afraid of owls. I have these two lifelike owls here." She reached for a plastic bag and produced two fluffy replicas. "When you're hanging up the gorse, I suggest that you also put one of these owls at either end of the church. With these two solutions, we're bound to get rid of them."

"I'll give it a try," said Bertie very half-heartedly. "But I'm not sure, not sure at all."

Maureen passed him the two fluffy owls.

***

Later that week, Charlie cut down some gorse bushes and, with the help of his sons, installed them along with the two owls.

When he next went to open the church for the evening service, the bat mess was as bad as ever, and dried gorse pins covered the floor.

He cursed roundly. It had doubled the work for himself and Hilda. The two owls looked down on them with a wise, superior, unwavering stare.

Chapter 40

As Jonathan was collecting his papers and saying good night to the members at the end of the meeting, he glanced at his phone and opened the message.

It was from Wendy Morris.

"Hi, Jonathan. I'm sure you didn't expect to be hearing from me, but in case you haven't heard, Laurence Finch is dead, murdered in a side street in Dublin. Call me if you like."

Jonathan drove back to the rectory, poured himself a stiff gin and tonic and phoned Wendy.

"Hi, Wendy. This is Jonathan Appleford. I hadn't heard about Laurence Finch. I'm down in the back of beyond and missed the news today. You say Laurence Finch was murdered? Gosh!"

Wendy told Jonathan what she had heard. "I don't know how close you were to him, but underneath the affable person he liked to portray, he wasn't a nice person. And I'm not basing that solely on my own experience of him in St. Olaf's School."

"Guy Morgan thought very highly of him. Treated him like his right-hand man and listened to his advice. I always felt uncomfortable in his company. It was like he was hiding something while at the same time looking for information to use against you."

"Yes, that would be him."

"In fact," Jonathan went on, "I'm sure Laurence Finch was behind my sudden departure from St. Stephen's."

And then the floodgates opened. Jonathan hadn't talked to anyone about his dismissal except Rosie. His supposed friend in the cathedral, Daniel Norton, had gone silent, not wanting to be tainted by association.

Jonathan told Wendy about going to the cathedral for evensong, his preference for good liturgy after his time in Cambridge and Liverpool, how he allowed himself to be sucked into going to The Bishop's Apron after evensong. "Laurence Finch was a regular at the cathedral and at drinks afterwards. He said he was a former choirboy, but he wasn't popular with the younger members of the cathedral choir I met, who had all sorts of unsavoury stories about him.

"I was invited to a party where there was lots of drink. Well, things got out of hand. Laurence Finch had been invited and didn't turn up, but he obviously heard what went on and told Guy Morgan. I think he was afraid that I was hearing too much about him and wanted me out of the way. It wasn't hard to turn Guy against me. He had come to the conclusion that I wasn't the true-blue evangelical he had appointed as curate. In that, he was correct. Cambridge changed me." He gave a hollow laugh. "And here I am in Inchymore. It's beautiful but a very lonely spot."

"Could I just say to you," Wendy said, "you will probably get a visit from DCI Frank Mulready, who's investigating the murder. I will not be telling him anything as a result of this conversation, but as Laurence Finch was a parishioner of St. Stephen's and you knew him, you will probably be contacted."

"Heavens! They don't think I murdered him?" Jonathan cried. "As if I haven't suffered enough already!"

Wendy must have sensed his panic because she assured him calmly, "No, I don't think they regard you as a suspect, but they might want some background information. It may never happen, but it's better to be prepared. Look, I've got to go. But feel free to ring me anytime."

"Thanks, Wendy," Jonathan was relieved at the offer. "And can I say thanks for coming to my institution service. Guy didn't encourage anyone to come—either parishioners or clergy. He said it was too far. And before you go, I'm sorry if anytime I met you I seemed a bit distant. Guy Morgan did a good hatchet job on you too."

Jonathan's mind was all over the place as he ended the call. He gulped down his drink and poured another one.

Chapter 41

DCI Frank Mulready did phone Jonathan and made an appointment to see him in Inchymore.

As Wendy had suggested, it seemed to be a background-gathering exercise on Laurence Finch. Jonathan was relieved that, as far as he could detect, he was not being implicated in the murder. He was able to account for his movements on the night in question, as he'd been with the churchwardens, going over the agenda for the vestry meeting the following night.

Summer ended and with the autumn came longer evenings with less to do. Jonathan began to feel the loneliness of living alone in an isolated part of the country. Whereas in St. Stephen's, the onset of autumn meant a very full programme of parish activities, it was not the same in a remote parish where congregations were small and the area was large.

From time to time, he was invited to a meal in parishioners' houses. As well as copious amounts of food, there was a copious amount of drink, with whiskey being the favourite after-dinner tipple. There were times when he couldn't remember driving home and, on one occasion, woke up the next morning to find that he had slept in the car outside the front door of the rectory.

Inchymore had very few weddings. Many of the girls went to Protestant boarding schools. The boys were likely to go to local secondary schools, needing to help on their parents' farm and inheriting it when their parents died. Many of the girls went on to the cities, either for work or to college. Few came back, even to get married in their home church.

An exception was Frances Daly, daughter of churchwarden, Charlie Daly, and his wife, Florrie. Frances had gone to the local secondary school in Inchymore and was employed as a receptionist in the surgery of the local GP. She was engaged to a local lad who ran a supermarket owned by his parents.

It would be a 'mixed marriage', something that, in former years, Protestants in particular would have tried to avoid. But those days had passed, and the rows about which faith children would be brought up in were a thing of the past, much to the relief of everybody.

Charlie and Florrie were delighted about the forthcoming wedding, which was to be held in the bride's church, Inchymore Parish Church, with Jonathan and the local Roman Catholic priest officiating.

The wedding was in late autumn. For Aidan, the groom, the busy tourist season would be over, and for the Dalys, the harvest would be finished and all would have been safely gathered in.

The Dalys were also glad that 'their own man' would be marrying them.

It was Jonathan's first wedding. In St. Stephen's, Guy Morgan liked to take all the weddings. "It's a missional opportunity," he told Jonathan. "A time to show St. Stephen's at its best and to preach a Christian message," inferring that was something he couldn't trust Jonathan to do. Guy used to boast to couples that St. Stephen's did the best weddings in Lislea, if not in Daneford diocese.

Knowing it was Jonathan's first wedding, Charlie and Florrie were not short of advice to give him at the rehearsal.

"The Canon used to precede the bride up the aisle," said Charlie.

"But the clergyman from next door waits for the bride and her father at the chancel steps." Florrie added to the confusion.

Jonathan didn't like the idea of the father 'giving away' his daughter. He remembered a conversation he had in Liverpool with Father Damien, who had stopped the practice because it smacked too much of the daughter being the property of her father. It wasn't in any of the revised liturgies, but Charlie insisted that it should be included. It would be his moment of glory in the service.

It was, Jonathan felt, not a battle worth fighting.

On the morning of the service, Jonathan was more nervous than the couple. He was on show. The reputation of the parish of Inchymore depended on him doing a good service.

His order of service was so annotated he was bound to make a mistake. His priest colleague was laid-back and amused by Jonathan's fussiness about the service.

He preached a short, amusing sermon, one that he had heard Father Damien preach in Liverpool, and to his relief, it went down well with the congregation.

His only other duty was to say grace at the wedding reception where he was seated at the end of the top table.

In the long wait before the meal while photographs were being taken, he was plied with drinks by guests, and the wine flowed freely during the meal. By the time the music started, he was feeling light-headed and had become a bit unsteady on his feet. He decided that the best course was to say his goodbyes and head home.

The cold air hit him as he left the hotel, and his head began to spin. He eventually found his car, flopped into the driving seat, and made his way as carefully as he could out of the car park and headed for Kilcadam rectory.

A half mile from home, a bright light shone in the centre of the road. Were his eyes playing tricks? Was it a motorbike coming up the centre of the road? He jerked to a halt. The light approached him and there was a knock on his window.

He wound it down, and though it was pitch-dark, the reflected light of a torch illuminated the unmistakeable uniform of a policeman, who poked his head through the window and shone the torch on Jonathan's face. He saw the dog collar.

"Ah, Father, is it yourself? Now, this is a small car you're driving, and it shouldn't take up all the road, and there's really no need to check out the far side of the road either. By the smell in the car, you've had a skinful! Now what have you to say for yourself before I take this further?"

The shock stunned Jonathan into sobriety. "I'm so sorry, Officer. I've been at a wedding. It was my first and I was so relieved everything went well that I probably had one too many."

"More than one too many by the way you're driving. By right, I should breathalyse you and take you to the station. But seeing who you are, I'm letting you off with a caution—this time. Now, Father, be a good boy. Get out of the car. I'll park it in this layby and then drive you home. You can come and collect your car tomorrow when you're sober. But mind, I won't be as kind the next time!"

Jonathan was driven home in the squad car. The policeman gave him his key ring. Jonathan fumbled to find the front door key and finally stumbled, relieved and embarrassed, into the rectory.

Chapter 42

THE INFORMATION ON Laurence Finch that DCI Frank Mulready was compiling from his interviews was in stark contrast to the glowing character reference that the Ven. Guy Morgan had given him when he went to see the archdeacon. In addition, there was the file he had compiled at the time of the murder of Ian Wilson, Wendy Morris's organist in St. Olaf's. It detailed the bad-tempered relationship Finch had with Wendy and with Ian Wilson, and his membership of the board of the Sunset Strip Gentlemen's Club.

Mulready's inquiries also led him to Daneford Cathedral. The dean was not at all pleased to be interviewed by the police over a former choirboy who was only an occasional member of the cathedral congregation. The dean tried to distance himself by pointing out that his duties were more administrative and strategic than pastoral and shuttled Mulready to his vicar, Daniel Norton, who had a pastoral role in the cathedral and looked after the choir.

In turn, Daniel Norton, admitted only to a passing acquaintance with Laurence Finch and directed the DCI to Nigel and Patrick in the choir, "...who seemed to know Mr. Finch a lot better and socialised with him."

Nigel and Patrick were flattered to be helping the police with their inquiries and were happy to dish the dirt on Laurence Finch.

"A bit of a man for pretty girls," volunteered Nigel. "I've seen him chatting up the choir ladies in The Bishop's Apron after evensong. And, well, his behaviour at some of the choir parties left a lot to be desired. He never got very far with any of the fair sex."

"Well, as far as we know," interrupted Patrick, giggling.

"None of the choir really liked him," continued Nigel. "He felt he had a right to come to gatherings because he had been a past member of the choir, though few of his contemporaries are still singing with us."

"And even they avoided him," added Patrick. "He came along even though not invited."

"I probably shouldn't say this," Nigel said, "but I heard down the grapevine that the same Laurence Finch had a predilection for minors. I can't prove it, but that's the gossip."

Trying to find a motive for Laurence Finch's murder, DCI Mulready wondered if, perhaps, the murder was the work of someone Finch had sexually abused at some time. There was no CCTV in the alley in which he had been found, and they hadn't found any witnesses. The only trace of the assailant was a footprint, which forensics said was made by an expensive running shoe. The pathologist confirmed that the cause of death was a blow from a blunt instrument.

***

DCI Frank Mulready phoned Wendy Morris and arranged a time to meet with her at her rectory.

"I have the coffee ready," she said as she ushered him into the kitchen. "What can I do for you?"

"I've learnt that there are rumours, unsubstantiated at the moment, that your deceased principal might have been involved in child sexual abuse. I'm just wondering if you ever heard anything about such allegations in your school?"

The question caught Wendy on the hop. She hesitated.

"Can I take that as a 'yes'?" asked the DCI.

"I know of one," said Wendy, reluctantly. "Now this is very awkward. One parent has confided in me about an incident involving Laurence Finch. While it doesn't come under the seal of the confessional, I don't want to break confidence, especially as it might affect the mental health and stability of the child concerned."

"I have to remind you that this is a murder investigation," Mulready countered.

"Yes, I know," replied Wendy. "But give me twenty-four hours, will you? I'll talk to the parent involved and try to get her cooperation. Can the child concerned be left out of any interview, at least at this stage?"

"I can't give any guarantees. We both know Laurence Finch was not the person he appeared to be. But a murder is a murder."

After Frank Mulready left, Wendy rang Ellie Jones and asked that if Mia and Noah could be left alone for an hour or, if a babysitter could be got, would she call at the rectory? "Something important has come up, and I need to talk to you."

Ellie said the children would be all right on their own for a while and she would be with Wendy in a few minutes.

Over a cup of coffee, Wendy brought Ellie up to date on police investigations and the unsubstantiated allegation about child sexual abuse.

"I got to know the DCI quite well over the murder of my organist, Ian Wilson, and I would trust him to keep Mia out of the questioning if at all possible. I think he just wants the child sexual abuse allegation confirmed so that he can follow up that aspect of the case. I can assure you that I haven't mentioned your name. It's up to you whether you want to speak to the DCI. All I can say is that your cooperation would greatly help Frank Mulready solve the case. Take your time. Sleep on it if you like."

Ellie fiddled with her spoon, turning it around and around in her hand, deep in thought.

With a decisive movement, she returned the spoon to the saucer. “OK. I will talk to the DCI and confirm the incident. But Mia must be left out of it. That is my only condition.”

Chapter 43

It was a horrible, wet morning when DCI Mulready and Detective Sergeant Julie Williams called to the home of Ellie Jones. They ran up the driveway to avoid getting a soaking. Ellie had phoned her office to say that she would be in late that morning.

"Good morning, Mrs. Jones. I'm DCI Frank Mulready and this is DS Williams," Mulready said as Ellie opened the door to them. "I really appreciate you seeing us at such short notice, and I understand you know why we are here."

Ellie showed them into the front room. "Wendy has filled me in on your investigation into the murder of Laurence Finch. But as I said to her, so I say to you now, I must first have your word that Mia will not be dragged into any of this. I think I have been very lucky that what she has experienced has not had a worse effect on her—at least as far as I can see—and I don't want to have to reopen what she went through.

" I do appreciate your concerns, Mrs. Jones. I just want to have some proof that the allegations of child sexual abuse by Laurence Finch are substantiated."

"I can tell you that he tried to kiss Mia and inappropriately touch her," Ellie said. Tears filled her eyes.

"When and where was this?" asked Mulready.

"It was here in this house."

"Here?" Mulready asked, puzzled.

"On the advice of Archdeacon Morgan. I was, at the time, a parishioner of St. Stephen's, and he suggested that Laurence

Finch could give Mia extra tuition. You see, me and my husband, Ollie—" She gestured to photos on the wall. "—we wanted Mia to go to the school we both attended. But when Ollie died, that became impossible financially. It's a fee-paying school, and the only way Mia could go there was if she was awarded a scholarship. Hence the extra tuition."

"And was Laurence Finch left alone with Mia?" asked the DCI.

"Not usually. I work part-time, and I made sure I was always home before the children returned from school. Except one day, I was late. I was involved in a car accident on the way home from the office. Someone ran into the back of me at traffic lights. It took ages to sort out. Mia and Noah have keys to the house, just in case, and I told them to let Laurence Finch in and I would get home as quickly as I could. But the other driver insisted on calling the police, and that's what caused the delay. That's when it happened. He was making his escape when I got home."

"Did Noah witness anything?" asked DS Williams.

"Noah usually went in next door to play with his pal, Joel McFall. Joel's father, Declan, works from home, and he kept an eye on the boys. It saved me from asking Noah to be quiet while the extra tuition was going on."

"What do you mean when you say Laurence Finch 'inappropriately touched' Mia?" the DS asked.

"He put his hand on her leg under her dress and moved it up to her private parts, trying to kiss her at the same time. When Mia realised what he was doing, she got up and ran from the room. She was going to go to Declan next door, but then I arrived home as Laurence Finch was leaving."

Just then, the doorbell rang and Ellie went to answer it. She was back in a minute.

"Sorry about that. In fact, it was Declan from next door. He saw my car outside and seeing I was still at home, he was wondering if I was OK." She paused. "Can I get you some tea or coffee?"

"No, thanks, all the same," replied Mulready. "You've been extremely helpful. I may have to talk to you again, but I will do my utmost to keep Mia out of it. I do understand your concerns."

With that, they got up and left. They were putting on their coats outside the front door when he noticed, on the tiles under the canopy, two footprints matching the design of the shoe that was found at the scene of the murder.

He took out his phone and photographed them. Turning to Ellie, who was still at the front door, he asked, "Would these be Declan's shoe prints?"

"Probably so. Declan's a keen runner. He goes for a run first thing in the morning and often late at night. He's very fussy about his running shoes and only buys the best. Why do you ask?"

"It's just an unusual design. My son is getting into running and wants to buy a proper pair of running shoes. If I can't get this type, I may have to ask your neighbour where he got them."

"I'm sure Declan would be only too glad to help. He's been a great neighbour, and Noah gets on really well with him. He's been like a surrogate father to him." She laughed. "They both share a very strong dislike for Laurence Finch. Declan was a pupil of Finch's many years ago, before he became principal of St. Olaf's."

"Well, we must get on," said DCI Mulready. "Thank you once again for your help."

Ellie put on her coat. "I'll walk out to the car with you. I have to get to the office. Here, shelter under this umbrella, this rain is awful. It's no use getting wet."

Chapter 44

RELIEVED THAT ELLIE was leaving at the same time as himself and DS Williams, the DCI drove straight back to HQ to compare his photo with the footprint they had found at the scene of the murder.

It was an exact copy. It was time to interview Declan McFall. Taking DS Williams with him, they drove back to Ellie's next-door neighbour.

The door was answered by Declan. He was wearing a T-shirt, tracksuit bottoms and trainers.

"Mr. Declan McFall? I'm DCI Mulready and this is DS Williams. May we come in?"

"What's this all about?" A worried look crossed Declan's face.

"We'd like to talk to you about Laurence Finch," replied Mulready. "I think it's best that we talk indoors rather than on the doorstep."

Declan brought them into the front room.

"My wife's at work and my son, Joel, is at school. I work from home." He indicated two easy chairs for the DCI and the DS to sit in but remained standing in front of the fireplace.

"Did you know Laurence Finch?" asked Mulready.

"I heard about him from Noah Jones. Noah came in to play with Joel when Mr. Finch was giving extra lessons to Mia. Ellie told us about the arrangements and how it would be easier if Noah wasn't around the house when the lessons were taking place. But he's often here. He and Joel are great pals."

"Did Noah say anything about Laurence Finch?" asked DS Williams.

"He certainly didn't like him. Thought Finch tried to be too nice—for a teacher. Noah doesn't particularly like school or teachers, so it wasn't surprising that he took against Mr. Finch."

"Did you have any contact with Laurence Finch?" DS Williams persisted.

"Me? No! I was just working in my office while the boys played—"

"Would you please take off your right shoe?" cut in the DCI.

Declan did as requested.

DS Williams produced a photocopy of the photo Mulready had taken outside Ellie's front door. She held it next to the trainer.

"An exact match, Sir," said DS Williams.

The DCI nodded and addressed Declan. "Can you explain why a print of your trainers was found at the scene of Laurence Finch's murder?"

"What?! That proves nothing!" Declan protested. "There must be hundreds of these trainers around."

"They're not a cheap make bought in any sports shop," countered the DCI. "They are a rather exclusive and expensive brand made for serious runners—like yourself, Mr McFall. We've checked. We have also checked local suppliers, and there is only one in this area. And we've also checked that you are a customer."

"Maybe so. But there are many others who would have bought this type of running shoe. They're popular with serious runners. Why pick on me?"

"Well, the interesting thing about this print is this." The DCI pointed to the heel part of the image. "There's a slight nick in the sole, like it was cut by a piece of glass. And there's a slight nick in your trainer at exactly the same place."

Declan was silent.

"We're going to take you to the station for questioning. You are not obliged to say anything, unless you wish to do so, but anything you say will be taken down in writing and may be given in evidence."

"I think I have a right to have a solicitor present," said Declan.

"Yes, you do," replied DCI Mulready. "We will wait here while you make the call. The station is in Lislea."

***

Despite the presence of a solicitor beside him, Declan was terrified as he sat facing DCI Mulready and DS Williams in the interview room. The solicitor told Declan that he didn't have to answer their questions and could just say 'no comment', which would give them time to fully discuss the accusation when the interview was over.

Having confirmed his name, address and age, Declan replied "No comment" to every question.

But the longer the interrogation went on, the more intimidated he felt. After two hours of intense, repetitive questioning with no response given except '"No comment," the interview was adjourned and he was taken to a cell.

Mulready and his team set to work and quickly established where Declan was born. From this, they were able to discover from the Department of Education that Laurence Finch had been a teacher in the primary school Declan would probably have attended. This was strong evidence that what Ellie had told them about Declan having been taught by Laurence Finch was true.

Time to continue the interview.

It was obvious that the whole ordeal was taking its toll on Declan McFall. His face was pale and drawn, and his eyes were bloodshot from crying.

"Mr. McFall, we have found that you were a pupil of Laurence Finch as a child." The DCI looked straight at him. "You lied to us when you said you only knew him from what Noah Jones had told you. We know that Laurence Finch abused at least one child in his care. Were there more? Were you one of them?"

Declan crumpled. Ignoring his solicitor's restraining arm, he replied, "Yes, I was one, and there were others, boys and girls. He would make us feel very special, give us treats, take us for drives in his car and...and...fiddle with us. We didn't know any better. He warned us not to tell our parents or it would be worse for us in class. He was very free with the cane in school, and we were afraid. Our parents thought he was great. So we said nothing. Who would have believed us? Nice Mr. Finch! So good to the pupils! Pillar of the church! Respected by everyone! And when Noah told me what he tried to do to Mia, it all came flooding back. He couldn't, he *shouldn't* be allowed to continue to mess up young people's lives. I followed him for weeks, got to know his routine and his attendance at that disgusting club in Dublin. He was a pervert. It had to end. I had to confront him."

"And hit him on the head with a blunt instrument," added DCI Mulready.

"No. I didn't hit him with anything. I pushed him and shoved him and shouted at him, that's all. I didn't have anything with me to hit him with."

"Did he fall when you pushed him?" asked DS Williams.

"No! He just stood there, laughing and sneering. His speech was slurred and he was obviously drunk. Told me I was always a wimp and a no-good. Said I should man up and hit him."

"And did you?"

Declan shook his head. "I lived up to his description of me and ran home."

"Did you see anyone else in the vicinity?" asked DCI Mulready.

"No, I don't think so. It was dark. And, anyway, at that stage, I was feeling so humiliated—Finch could do that to you—that all I wanted to do was get away."

Mulready's phone rang and he left the room. A minute later, he opened the door and called DS Williams to join him.

Chapter 45

"Where are we going?" asked DS Williams as they got into Mulready's car.

"To St. Stephen's and the Venerable Guy Morgan," replied the DCI.

"Whatever for?" asked the surprised Detective Sergeant.

"That was the pathologist. They've determined that the blunt instrument was made of wood. They have also recovered a splinter from Finch's scalp. And, most interestingly of all, they reckon that the blow which killed Laurence Finch happened at least twenty-four hours before he died."

"Where does the archdeacon come into all of this?"

"It's only a hunch at the moment, but let's see how this goes."

They reached St. Stephen's rectory. Guy Morgan opened the door.

"Ah. DCI Mulready, we meet again!"

"May we come in?" asked the DCI.

Guy Morgan led them into the hallway and closed the front door.

"I have a few more questions about Laurence Finch's death. Can we go into your study?"

"Of course," Guy said. "Will this take long? I do have a meeting to go to in a few minutes' time."

Guy sat behind his desk and motioned Mulready and Williams to sit in two armchairs opposite.

"When was the last time you saw Laurence Finch?" asked DCI Mulready.

"Eh, let me see." Guy Morgan opened his diary. "Actually, it was late afternoon on the day before he was so tragically murdered."

"And where did you meet him?"

"Here in the rectory. In fact, he sat on the chair you're sitting on."

"And, may I ask, what was the purpose of his visit?"

Morgan hesitated. "It was on personal and parish business. I'd rather not discuss it."

"I'm afraid you will have to. Or else we can do it more formally in the station."

"Well, in that case..." Guy Morgan spread his hands flat on the desk on front of him. "It had come to my attention that Mr. Finch was not the person I thought he was."

"Oh?"

"I was told that he was a member of some lewd gentlemen's club in Dublin, actually on their board, and that..." He paused. "There was a rumour going round that he had engaged in paedophilia."

"And how did you come across that information?"

"I happened to be preaching in the cathedral the day before. It was my turn on the rota. The dean and I don't see eye to eye on matters of doctrine and liturgy. The dean is one of those wishy-washy liberals who interpret the scriptures to suit themselves. A few days previously, there had been a diocesan meeting to discuss same-sex blessings. It's a topic that is dividing the church at the present time."

"Yes, I know," Mulready said impatiently.

"At that meeting, I had argued forcibly—and cogently, I might add—that we should be faithful to what was clearly written in the Bible and not be accommodating ourselves to present-day opinions. Well, in our discussion in the chapter room after the service, the dean accused me of being a hypocrite."

"Oh?"

"He asked how I could hold such a strict position when one of my most prominent parishioners was a member of a girlie club, chased after women at parties and was probably a paedophile.

"I was speechless and denied having such a person in my parish. I asked him to identify the person in question. Then he told me, with a great deal of satisfaction, that it was Laurence Finch. I couldn't believe it! He was my biggest supporter, my right-hand man."

"How had the dean come across this information?" asked DS Williams.

"From his vicar, Daniel Norton, who got it on good authority from members of the choir. He hangs around with them quite a lot, goes drinking with them after services and goodness knows what else.

"So, I rang Laurence Finch and asked him to call here on his way home from school the following day. I confronted him with what I had been told."

"And how did he respond?" asked Mulready.

"Of course, he denied it at first. Asked where I had heard such rubbish. And when I told him that it had come from the cathedral and from members of the choir, he became quiet. I assumed then that it must, at least, be partly true. I then told him that he could no longer be a parishioner of St. Stephen's and that he must resign from the Select Vestry and other committees. He got up out of his chair and approached my desk. I have never seen him so angry."

"And?"

"I told him that I couldn't have my reputation and that of St. Stephen's be associated with such behaviour and dragged through the mud. I told him that all connections with St. Stephen's must be severed forthwith. I stood up to signal the end of the meeting, and he grabbed me by the lapels of my jacket. He was seething with anger. His eyes were bulging. I thought he was going to punch me."

"What did you do?" asked the DCI.

"I…I…reached behind me and grabbed my old cricket bat and hit him before he could hit me. He staggered a bit, looking dazed and confused, so I took the opportunity to grab him and push him out of the front door. He stumbled towards his car, and I closed the door."

"What did you do then?" asked Williams.

"I went into the kitchen, made a cup of tea to steady my nerves, and when I looked out of the window, he had gone."

"Was there anyone else here in the rectory at the time?" asked Mulready.

"No! My wife, Faith, was at a parish meeting. She didn't come home until much later."

"I will have to take your old cricket bat in for forensic examination. Have you something I could wrap it in?"

As Guy Morgan went away to get a black sack, Mulready lifted the bat off the wall, holding the handle in his handkerchief. He noticed that the sides were rough. It also looked cleaner than when he had seen it on his last visit. It had obviously been scrubbed.

"Was there much blood? You must have hit him with a great deal of force."

"I was incensed. To think he had done all that to me and St. Stephen's. I suppose I did hit him hard. But he was OK—well, he was alive when he left the rectory. I didn't kill him," said Guy Morgan defiantly.

DS Williams took the bat from the DCI and slipped it into the black sack.

"We'll be in touch," said Mulready. "However, I must insist that you do not leave the country and that you remain in the rectory until we contact you."

As they made their way to the front door, the archdeacon followed them. "Laurence Finch was alive when he left here. He may have been a bit groggy, but he was able to drive away. He didn't collapse. You can't accuse me of being responsible for his death!"

Chapter 46

When presented with the forensic and medical evidence of Laurence Finch's death, the Ven. Guy Morgan, in an effort to salvage something of his own and his parish's shattered reputations, pleaded guilty to manslaughter. He was treated leniently and given a suspended sentence. He resigned his orders and moved to a quiet, rural town far away from Lislea and Daneford diocese.

Declan McFall was released from Lislea police station. He later joined an abuse survivors' group and became one of their most outspoken advocates. He continued to be an influential part of Noah Jones's life and a good neighbour to Ellie.

The bishop appointed the Revd. Wendy Morris as archdeacon of Daneford, much to the delight of the clergy in Daneford.

Down in Inchymore, Jonathan Appleford's late-night brush with the police served as a wake-up call. He couldn't go on as he was doing. He realised that he needed help and went to see the bishop, Andrew Caldwell, and poured out his heart.

The bishop was far more understanding and forgiving than Jonathan thought he would be. He arranged counselling for Jonathan at diocesan expense. It would be well outside the diocese and would be confidential.

Lonely though the parish of Inchymore could be, Jonathan threw himself into both the parish and the community, both of whose activities filled many of his evenings. He determined that he would pay a visit to Father Damien in Liverpool, and certainly, as a matter of priority, he would go and see Rosie.

About Ted Woods

I am a retired priest of the Church of Ireland, now living in Liverpool.

I served in a number of parishes in Ireland, North and South, most latterly in Rathfarnham, Dublin. I was a General Synod member, a Director of Ordinands, and worked in The Theological College looking after intern deacons in their final year.

For many years, I wrote a column on ministry for the *Church of Ireland Gazette*. For five years before retirement, I wrote a weekly 'soap'—'Down in St. David's'—for the *Gazette* about the ups and downs of clerical life. On my retirement, another writer took over.

I have self-published a book on Kindle—*And Some There Were*—a light look at 'the Good, the Bad and the Ugly' in the clergy of the Church of Ireland's past. The book includes twenty-five sketches, historically accurate, of priests and prelates from Reformation times to the twentieth century. With the aim of informing and entertaining, *And Some There Were* features the rogues as well as the righteous, the murdered and the murdering, priests and bishops alike.

Deacon is my third fictional novel, a sequel to *Bishop* and *Priest*.

By the Author

And Some There Were:
Sketches of some Irish Anglican Prelates and Priests

Bishop

Priest

Deacon

Beaten Track Publishing

For more titles from Beaten Track Publishing,
please visit our website:

http://www.beatentrackpublishing.com

Thanks for reading!

Printed in Great Britain
by Amazon

41050830R00081